PAUL BRADSHAW was born in Dublin and refuses point blank to grow up. He took up writing in order to tell ghost stories at summer camps but got into trouble when the kids started having bad dreams. He has since turned to writing humour and is having much more fun. The kids, though, still have bad dreams.

He's into painting, especially faces, collects metal badges and spends far too much time on the internet.

Circle of Suspicion is the sequel to *Circle of Daredevils*, his first book

GU00801692

Paul Bradshaw

Circle of Suspicion

THE CHILDREN'S PRESS

To Mum, Dad and Tracy –
in the hope they'll read
this one!

First published 2002 by
The Children's Press
an imprint of Anvil Books
45 Palmerston Road, Dublin 6

1 3 5 6 4 2

ISBN 1 901737 39 X

Typeset by Computertype Limited
Printed by Colour Books Limited

Contents

1 The Bad News

It wasn't just hot in Five Rivers, it was sweltering. The sun can bake a place, fry it or boil it, but this was the first time it had ever tried to microwave one. Even the trees were beginning to sweat and most ice-cream men had taken the day off.

At the top of a cliff overlooking the bay sat Sean Redmond and Cara Ryan, two members of the old Circle of Daredevils. Having found an ice-cream man who was actually working, they'd made the most of it and were just polishing off their second double-chocolate screwball.

Sean looked down at the beach and the day trippers below. 'Looks like a giant anthill that's just been stepped on,' he said.

'Ever seen a giant anthill that's just been stepped on?'

'No.'

'Then how do you know what it looks like?'

That was Cara all over – query everything. 'Okay, okay,' he said. 'It looks like a nice long beach with lots of people.'

It was going to be a good summer, he thought confidently. For once. Make a change from the back-to-back piano recitals and the endless visits to boring relations that usually spoilt his summer. Now he had the Circle to do things with. This would be a real summer, new style. It was going to be long and hot and he was going to love every minute of it. Not since his father had died three years ago – also at the start of a summer, ironically – had he felt so full of ENTHUSIASM.

Suddenly Cara's phone bleeped. She pulled it out, then told him that Troy and Niamh were at the bottom of the hill and would be up in a few minutes.

Sean smiled. 'Niamh phoned to say that?'

'Nah, text message,' Cara said handing him her phone.

AT BOTM OF HLL. B W/U N 2:-)

'You can read that?'

'"At bottom of hill – be with you in two." Two minutes. Finishing with a smiley face – she always does that.'

'A smiley face? Where?'

'After the "N". It's an emoticon,' Cara told him. 'Don't you know what emoticons are?' She turned the phone sideways so that the two dots looked like eyes, the dash became a nose and the bracket turned into a smile.

'Oh yeah, I see it now,' Sean said.

'I can make it wink too. Look....'

She punched a few more buttons and handed the phone to Sean. He turned it sideways again.

This time it read: ;-)

'And surprise: :-0'

'And the classic: ~(_8'(1)'

'*What?*'

'Looks like Homer Simpson. Someone sent it to me a few days ago.'

Again Sean turned the phone sideways. 'Oh yeah! That's so cool!'

Cara turned off the display and put the phone back in her pocket.

Seconds later, a blonde-haired girl with a grin and a slightly smaller boy with a more suspicious-looking smile on his face dropped their bikes on the grass and collapsed beside them.

Niamh and Troy Sheridan had arrived.

Cara turned back to Sean. 'So how come you don't have a mobile phone?'

'My Mum thinks they cause brain cancer,' he said evasively. She also thought having a mobile would result in him being mugged or even killed, but the brain cancer excuse was less embarrassing. 'I think she read about it in *The Star.*'

'But doesn't she have a mobile?'

'Yeah, but she only uses it for emergencies.'

'Don't worry. You're better off without them,' Troy said. 'I don't have one either.'

That might be true, but Troy probably still knew what all the emoti-thingies meant, Sean thought to himself. And how to send a text message. He couldn't help feeling a bit isolated.

'I told Matt not to get me one,' Troy continued, referring to his father. 'Unlike some people,' he said, glaring at Cara and Niamh, 'I can live without them. I doubt you can phone from Australia anyway.'

'Oh yeah,' Niamh said suddenly, 'did you hear the news?'

'What news?'

Sean looked at her. He had the horrible feeling in his stomach that he wasn't going to like this...

'Matt got that writing job with the *National Geographic* and we're going to Australia,' she said calmly. 'On Thursday next. For five weeks. While he does his research.'

Five weeks? Suddenly, black clouds closed in on Sean's summer. And the sun had gone in behind one.

'So it looks like it's just you and Cara then,' Troy joked. 'How romantic...'

'Me and Sean?' Cara cut in, before Sean could give Troy a good shove. 'I'm off to London on Monday, remember?'

London...? Don't tell me I'm stuck on my own, Sean thought. Again...

'Yeah, Da's got a part in some musical in the West End, so me and Jake are going over with him for a few weeks.'

Sean opened his mouth and then closed it

again. They were all off on foreign trips like politicians on St Patrick's Day, the lucky sods.

'Never mind,' Niamh said, throwing a comforting arm over his shoulders. 'You can always terrorise Mr Kerr.'

All on his own? Now what was the point in terrorising the teacher they loved to hate all by himself? Where was the fun in that?

'You can't,' Cara said. 'He's won a place on that safari game show. If he doesn't get eaten or isn't voted off he'll win half a million. Hope he does.'

'You hope he *wins?*' Sean said.

'Yeah, it'd be cool. Then he'd give up teaching.'

Now there was a good point if ever he heard one. He really must keep an eye on the telly.

Just then, Niamh's mobile rang.

'Hello?… Oh, hi Vinnie…'

Vinnie? Who was Vinnie?

'You made it okay?… Cool! Well, guess what… we're going to Australia!… No, not all of us – only Troy and me. Cara's going to London for a few weeks, but you'll have Sean.'

She put the phone to her shoulder and said to Sean, 'It's okay, you'll like him. He's from Los Angeles.'

'That doesn't mean anything.'

'He's Keith's cousin.'

It was a good thing he wasn't holding anything, because if he had been, he'd have thrown it at her. He'd already spent several months being humiliated by Keith Adams, president of the Circle of Daredevils. And now he was going to be stuck with the dopey prat's cousin? Were they doing this deliberately?

'I don't think he's as bad as Keith,' Troy said.

'You've met him?'

'Not exactly, but we've been chatting with him on the net. Niamh's in love with him.'

'I am not,' Niamh said, looking up briefly from her phone. She said one last good-bye and hung up. 'How could I fall in love with someone I've never met?'

'Then why did you tell him that Cara really fancied Keith?' Troy cut in. 'Sounded like you were saving him for yourself?'

'She told him *what?*' Cara said. 'Someone is gonna die before I go anywhere…'

Seconds later, Niamh's phone bleeped. 'Oh look – he's sending me flowers, now!'

'What?'

@—>—>— —<—<—@

'See? The first part's the petals, then the stem, with two sets of leaves,' Cara explained to Sean.

'How romantic,' Niamh cooed.

Sean was about to say something to her when her phone bleeped again. He was beginning to understand exactly why Troy hated the things. This time it said: I O U 1 THUMPIN!

'What's that?' said Sean.

Niamh just typed in a few letters: BT HEZ QT!

'Cute? But who's cute?' asked Sean. He was beginning to catch on.

Cara's phone bleeped. Everyone looked from one end of the bench to the other.

'You're texting each other from... beside each other?' Troy said. 'Do you have any idea how pathetic you are?'

'What's so pathetic about being up to date?' Niamh smiled.

'You should really try a few days without a phone – it's called "living".'

Suddenly, the clock on the amusement arcade chimed out.

'Right, that's me out of here,' said Cara getting up. 'See you later.'

'We'd better get back too,' Niamh said.

'So I'm to be left here on my own?' said Sean. 'Some summer this is going to be.'

'You'll probably love it. Remember Hazlitt: "I am never less alone than when alone."'

Sean just stared at her. 'I can't believe you're quoting Kerr's favourite writer during the summer holidays,' he groaned as they got their bikes and followed Cara down the grassy heath. 'I'll bet he died alone, too.'

2 The Blues

What a prospect, thought Sean that evening.

Thursday, Niamh had said, and then they were off. For over a month. By the time they'd get back, he'd be off to his aunt in Dundalk for a week or two (it was the closest he ever got to a holiday) and when he got back, they'd practically be starting school again.

He could see it all before him now. Days stretching out endlessly with the same things happening again and again. Apart from getting up and going to bed, meals, piano practice and the monthly highlight of a piano recital for Mum's friends, there was nothing to fill the days.

Come on, think! he thought to himself. There have to be some options.

Okay, let's see.

Option one: go shopping with Mum. Nope, to be avoided at all costs unless he wanted to hang around endlessly while she chatted with strings of friends.

Option two: go swimming. There was a swimming gala coming up. On the other hand, the pool had gotten even colder and even dirtier lately. Just thinking about it made him shiver.

Option three: go and see Mrs O'Hare. Might hang on to that one, actually.

Option four: go for walks. Where? He'd seen everything there was to see. Over and over.

Option five: call a friend. Who? Joey – no, he put him down even more than Keith did. Mark – no, he was always into something different, skateboarding being the latest craze. Scruffy – yuck – I'm not that desperate.

And that was it. The only other alternatives were either watching TV or reading a book. *Lord of the Rings* should kill a few weeks.

It all boiled down to the fact, Sean concluded, that summer is no fun when you're on your own. He'd come to rely on Niamh, Troy and Cara and now they were gone. Even Keith – come back, Keith, all is forgiven – was better than nothing.

The summer was over and it hadn't even started yet.

'Are you going to play or what?'

Sean woke up suddenly. 'Oh, sorry, Grandad,' he said, looking down at the Scrabble board as if it had just materialised in front of him. He could have sworn Grandad had fallen asleep again. Wouldn't be the first time, but at least he wasn't driving this time.

Having Grandad to stay with them for the summer had its advantages because it took some of Mum's attention away from him.

Only some, unfortunately. Often when he was sneaking out on his way to Sheridans, in the pathetic belief that she was completely absorbed in chatting to Grandad about the gold old (pre Sean) days, there would be a strident, 'Where are you going, Sean?'

Still, on a one to ten scale, Grandad rated about four for diverting attention. Not too bad!

'Your turn,' reminded Grandad.

Sean thought for a few seconds, frowned, pushed around a few tiles on his rack and finally put three of them down on the board.

Grandad took one look at them and went even redder than he already was. 'What the bloody hell is that?' he complained. '"Txt" is not a word!'

'Yes it is,' Sean said. 'And it's worth thirty-seven points – the X is on a triple letter.'

Grandad looked down at the board, then at Sean. 'Really?' he said. He took a sip of Guinness and stared right into Sean's eyes. 'And what exactly does "txt" mean?'

'A text message. A… em… a message sent on a mobile phone – a text message, only it's spelt T-X-T,' Sean told him. 'People use it all the time.'

'Really?' Grandad shook his head. 'I'm being conned here, I just know it. No wonder you couldn't find a dictionary. Very convenient. Any-way, I didn't think you had a mobile phone.'

'I don't. My friends told me about it.'

'Right-o then.' Grandad shuffled some of the letters on his rack and finished the dregs of his Guinness. Then he put on his thoughtful face, peered down at his rack and settled in for a good think.

That should be it for a while, Sean figured. Grandad always took ages to play, especially when he was losing. He didn't take losing very well.

Sean used the time to think as well. About a mobile. He'd really have to get one. Did Mum not realise that he was the only person in the gang – in the world, really – who didn't have one? (Troy didn't count – he had opted not to have one). Not that it would be wise to mention the Sheridans – she put the them down as a 'bad influence' and Cara not much better.

'You don't need one,' she always said, which was beside the point. Nobody actually *needed* a mobile, people just had them. No, he'd have to appeal to her better instincts. Something along the lines of, 'If I fell down a cliff, how could I let you know I was in trouble?'

No, she'd probably just ban him from walking anywhere near a cliff edge.

How about her music circle? 'I'll play for them twice a month if you get me a mobile.' No, she expected him to play Beethoven and Bach for her friends without having to lay on bribes.

'CRAP!' yelled Grandad.

Mum, who had just come in with her mobile in one hand and a dishcloth in the other, nearly went white. 'Grandad!'

'C-R-A-P,' Grandad smiled. 'C on a double letter, P on a triple word... thirty-three... ten extra for turning "each" into "reach"... ha! Puts me in the lead by nine.'

Mum looked down at the board and sighed. 'You can't let Sean see that word.'

Probably thinks I've never heard it before, Sean thought. Where does she think I live? On the moon?

'Why not? Legitimate word,' Grandad said.

'I'm challenging it, anyway,' Sean said. 'It's a slang word and you're not allowed to use slang.'

'It's in the dictionary, added in the nineteen ninety-seven edition,' Grandad said. 'You find me one and I'll show you where it is. After you've shown me "txt". Now, it's your turn, and make it snappy because I'm getting tired.'

Later, Sean headed across the beach on the first of the long lonely walks that he was probably going to have to get used to. Usually, he would have called up to Sheridans but that seemed pointless now. Better get used to the solitary life.

Halfway to nowhere he came across a large rock jutting out of the sand and sat down. He looked at his watch; he would give himself five minutes of staring out to sea.

'Now there's a face that could stop a clock on a slow day,' a voice said suddenly. 'Or have you just heard a long-range weather forecast?'

Sean looked up. A small grey-haired woman with a face that had seen many years smiled back at him.

'Oh, hi Mrs O'Hare,' Sean replied. 'Just bored.'

A long walk *and* Mrs O'Hare in one day – and to think he'd been trying to keep the highlights spaced out in order to conserve them.

'Bored? No way a kid like you should be bored at the start of summer,' Mrs O Hare said. 'Where are your friends from the Circle of Daredevils? What dares are you thinking up? You should be full of plans right now.'

Not for the first time, Sean wondered how these old dears seemed to know what was going on anywhere at any given time. Aloud, he said, 'They're all going away for the summer. Everyone. Except me. I was thinking of calling up and maybe going on one of your ghost-hunts...?'

'Can't until autumn. I'll be in Brittany.'

Great! Sean gave a twisted smile. Another one going off. Here he was, young and fresh and stuck in Five Rivers, while even the pensioners were heading off for faraway places. At this rate, he'd have the whole place to himself – literally.

'Mont St Michel,' she said. 'Remember I told you about it – famous monastery that gets cut off when the tide comes in.' She laughed. 'Sounds familiar, I'll bet?'

'I remember,' Sean said. It had only been a few months since he and Cara had been cut off on an island when they had had to rescue Troy. He remembered the race across the sands as the sea surged in towards them and the wild dash to escape the angry white-flecked waves. Even thinking about it made him shudder.

'Anyway, I'll bring you back a t-shirt with something silly written in French on it. Right now though, I'd better get back. My friend said she'd phone at about nine.' As she turned she said, 'Don't worry too much about the summer – something always shows up.'

Sean smiled as he waved back. He wished he shared her optimism.

Well, he could cross option number three off his list.

3 The Good News

Things didn't look much better the next morning and as far as he was concerned they could only get worse.

Out in the hall, he could hear Mum cheerfully rounding up her musical circle for a spot of 'Bach and Biscuits' as she was calling it. Then, in a pause between calls while she checked her list, the phone rang.

'Hello, Redmonds!' Her voice couldn't have been any sweeter. Pause. Sigh of disapproval. 'Yes, he is. One second, I'll get him.'

She came into the front room where Sean was watching a film in murky black and white about the lives and loves of the two-toed (not to be confused with the three-toed) sloth and handed him the phone. 'It's for you. And I need it back, so please be quick.'

'If I had a mobile, you wouldn't have been interrupted,' said Sean.

'Don't be cheeky.'

'Hiya,' Sean said into the phone, 'who's there and what's up?'

'It's Niamh and we're *not* going to Australia.'

Sean sat up. 'You're not? That's brill! No, I

mean I'm sorry you're not going. It's a pity.'

'Don't worry about it,' Niamh laughed. 'I don't mind. I'll get to go some other time. Five weeks is a bit much anyway.'

'You're telling me!'

He looked up and saw Mum tapping her wrist.

'Anyway, we're meeting Vinnie down at Stella's in a few minutes. Want to come along?'

'Yeah, sure. I'll be there. Listen, I have to go. Mum wants the phone and...'

'Get a mobile.'

'I'm trying! Look, see you in a bit, okay?' He handed the phone back to Mum

'You're not going out in that, are you?' she asked as she peered through the window. Rain lashed against it as a grim reminder that summer could never be taken for granted.

Sean dashed out into the hall and grabbed an umbrella. He opened it just in case she thought he wasn't serious, and stepped out into the wonderful, wonderful rain and vanished.

Suddenly, everything was all right again. It could rain all season long if it wanted to, he couldn't give a toss. In his own personal summer, it was thirty degrees and climbing.

It was getting him wet, though. He legged it down the small arcade to Stella's, ducked in out of the rain, shook the water off his coat and folded up the umbrella.

'Ah sure, Seanie-boy, how a'ya?'

'Hi, Marco,' Sean beamed, picking up a nearby leaflet. 'What's this?'

'We're taking orders by text message now. Some people find it easier – mainly the ones that can't spell. Your friends are down th' back, same as usual.'

Sean tucked the ad in his pocket, said thanks and headed down to their normal table.

Then he saw them. Troy on one side, Niamh on the other, and a tall kid with long scraggy blond hair in the middle. He had teeth that looked like they shone in the dark and the most amazing pair of sunglasses he'd ever seen in his life. A single strip of reflective blue semi-transparent blue Perspex that stretched from ear to ear. They must have cost over a hundred euro.

This must be Vinnie, he thought.

He made his way over to the table as slowly as possible. Niamh was laughing so much she was having trouble drinking her coke. Every time she went to sip from the straw, Vinnie dug her in the ribs and made her splutter.

Sean hated him already.

Vinnie looked up as he reached the table and nearly blinded him with a smile. 'Hey, dude, you must be… Sean? Keith's told me all about you.'

'I deny everything,' Sean said.

Much to his surprise, Vinnie laughed.

'We were just talking about what we should do for the summer,' Niamh told him. 'Now that we're staying put.'

'Maybe we could start another Circle of Daredevils?' Sean suggested hopefully.

'Nah,' Troy said. 'Done that. Anyway, it wouldn't be the same with Kerr out in Africa.'

Pity, Sean thought. Ever since the Circle of Daredevils fell apart, he'd been missing it. Aloud, he said, 'There's a project on in the library – find your ancestors.'

'Shouldn't be too difficult, they're all dead. They don't get about much these days. Anyway, we don't have any here – we're immigrants, not like you.'

'Immigrants? You come from Wicklow!'

'There's that bowling tournament on up at the leisure centre. Could try and enter.'

'Nah,' Troy replied. 'We'd never win. Not if Stephen Henderson goes in for it – he got one of those brand new two-hundred-euro bowling balls that just blasts the pins away. He gets a strike nearly every time.'

'Too expensive, anyway,' Sean agreed. Then he asked Vinnie, 'So what would you be doing in LA?'

'Well, we usually hang out at the beach if nothing's happening. We're used to really hot weather over there, dude. Or we go shopping –

got some really mondo malls you can just get lost in. Not like over here. Or we watch whatever movies are being made. Follow the stars around.'

'Well, this isn't Los Angeles and there aren't any movies being made and it's still raining out there, I mean here,' Sean said, a little angrily. Suddenly, he began to feel a little bit of pride in Five Rivers. It might not be Los Angeles, but it wasn't the dump Vinnie was making it out to be.

'You know what I think we should do?' Vinnie said.

They all looked at him hopefully. If he comes up with something I haven't thought of, Sean raged, I'll kill him.

Vinnie sat forward in the chair and smiled. 'Well, you know the way that all these really cool seaside towns have, like, mysteries and stuff?'

'Ye-ah…?'

'We should find out your local mystery and sort it out!'

Sean looked at him. This guy had seen way too many X-files.

'I hate to disappoint you, but there aren't any mysteries around here,' Niamh said. 'If there were, we'd know about them.'

'What about, like, murders?'

The smiling was beginning to make Sean nervous. Was he going to suggest that they actually murder someone and then play cat-and-mouse with the police?

'This isn't New York,' Troy laughed. 'We'd be spoilt for choice in New York.'

'But I'm not from New York, man.'

Sean couldn't resist the opportunity. He put his thumbs together to form a 'W' and said slowly, 'What-ever…'

'No, wait a sec,' Niamh said. 'Could be some-thing there. Think Great Train Robbery?'

Sean frowned. What did that have to do with Five Rivers? They didn't even have a train station.

'It was on the Discovery channel a few days ago. Bunch of English guys in the sixties robbed this mail train and made off with a couple of million or so. They hid out in some tiny little village intending to lie low. They figured that the police would only check the big cities like London and large towns, but not the villages.'

'So they got away with it?'

'No, they attracted too much attention from the locals. Four strangers coming in and out of a barn in a village where everyone knows everyone else? Highly suspicious. Someone called the police in the end and they got caught.'

'Told you, guys,' Vinnie said. 'Every little town has a secret – even if it doesn't know it. We'll scan the local papers for anything weird and then keep an eye on it. We'd have to split up a bit, or we'd be the ones standing out.'

'What... you mean on our own?' asked Troy.

'No, in pairs. And meet back somewhere in the evenings.' Vinnie turned to Troy and Niamh. 'Your tree-house would be perfect.'

'So what's the first step? Who goes with who?' Sean said, hoping that he'd be teamed up with Niamh. Could it happen...?

'We'll draw lots,' said Vinnie briskly. He tore up one of Marco's ads into four strips of different lengths and folded them tightly into scraws. 'The two longest are one team and the two shortest are the other.'

'Who goes first?'

'Clockwise, I guess,' Vinnie replied. 'Niamh first, then me, then Sean and then Troy.'

Niamh and Vinnie took a scraw each leaving Sean with two choices. He chose one, paused, changed his mind and then picked the other. Wouldn't have mattered which, because when they had all been unravelled Niamh and Vinnie had the two shortest and he and Troy had the two longest.

So he'd be teamed up with Troy for most of the summer, and Troy, judging by the snort he gave, didn't like the idea in the first place.

'So that's it settled, then, dudes,' Vinnie said, looking up. 'And sign of that pizza? We ordered it ages ago.'

4 Clifftop House

'Are you sure you want to go out for a walk, father? It's awfully wet out there,' Mum said.

It was a lifetime later and Sean was back at home, thinking. Of course Vinnie must have engineered the whole thing. Question was: how?

'I'll be fine,' Grandad replied. 'No one gets healthier sitting inside watching an idiot box. Besides, Sean's going to keep me company.'

'I am?'

'Of course you are. Now grab a coat and let's move. It's not getting any wetter out there.'

Sean looked at Mum. There was no way he fancied going out again. Once was enough on a day like this. For what seemed like the first time in his life, was she going to be on his side?

Then she hesitated. 'Father, if you're sure...'

'What...?' Sean gasped. 'But I don't...'

But resistance was futile. He trudged out to the hall, muttering under his breath. The one time he needed her to say 'no' she went and stuck up for Grandad. Was she doing it on purpose?

Outside, it was still warm and it was still wet. They headed down to the main street. 'Ah, I remember this place back when it was a country village,' Grandad said as he stabbed at the button on the traffic lights with the end of the umbrella. 'The sun, the sea, the candy-floss, the smugglers, the gun-running up at Clifftop House....'

Sean woke up. 'The what?'

'Gun-running. It was a secret back then, but everyone knew about it.'

Some secret, Sean thought.

A black car eased up to the lights just as they were about to cross, then the driver put a foot down. It came so close to Sean that he stepped back, lost his footing and landed in a puddle.

Grandad shook his fist at the driver. 'What the hell is wrong with you, you colour-blind moron?' he yelled.

The driver slammed on the brakes.

'Oh, you wanna piece of me, now do you?' Grandad yelled. 'Come on over and take what you can, just bring some ID for the ambulance.'

The car stopped for a second, then revved up and accelerated off into the distance, leaving Sean, soaked to the skin, to pick himself up.

'Lunatic,' Grandad said. 'Did you see the huge dent in the side of the car? He's hit something before. Did you get the number, by the way?'

Typical! fumed Sean. I'm nearly run over and he's asking me whether I noticed a dent in the side of the car and had I got the number. What was he doing? But all he said was, 'No.'

'Pity.'

'Did you?'

'Can't see without my specs,' Grandad said. 'Are you all right?'

'Yeah, I think so...'

'Good. Well, come on, then – we came for a walk, not a sit-down.'

As they crossed the road, Sean realised that it had actually stopped raining. Down on the beach, giant puddles covered most of the sand and it was like walking across a wet sponge.

'Where were we? Yes. Clifftop House.'

Sean looked up at the gaunt framework of the house that had been there for as long as he could remember. A spooky-looking slightly off-balance house, with gaping crooked walls and windows. It was supposed to be haunted, but no one knew why or by whom.

'We were forbidden to go anywhere near the place, pain of death,' Grandad rambled on, 'so naturally enough, we were up there all the time. Woman called Mad Sheila used to own it. That was until she was killed in an explosion. Box of grenades they smuggled in from Brazil. Some eejit took a pin out to see if they worked. When it didn't go off he put it back in the box. Killed nine people, he did. Everyone in the house.'

'What did she want grenades for?'

'No idea. I was never daft enough to ask her. Maybe they were Trotskyites?'

Sean knew better than to ask what a Trotskyite was. If there was one thing this dank damp evening could do without, it was a lecture. But there was no stopping Grandad. 'It was used by real smugglers in the old days.'

'Smugglers? Here?'

'You get smugglers everywhere you get caves and small towns,' Grandad said. 'Mainly brandy and wine in those days, or guns and ammunition. They used to run the boats right up into the cliffs – there would have been steps up to the house.'

Sean wasn't really listening. He was looking up at the old house. As he did a light came on, which was odd. It went off and then came on again.

'There's a light on up there now,' he said. 'I thought no one lived there any more?'

'Oh, no one could live there now. That whole place is unsafe, just waiting for a cave-in,' Grandad said, squinting at the house. 'Must be your eyesight. Or some sort of reflection from the sunset.'

'Cool!' Sean smiled to himself. He looked up at Clifftop House again. There was no sunset – it was too cloudy and, anyway, the house was facing east. He had definitely seen a light.

Maybe Vinnie was right about little seaside towns and mysterious secrets.

5 Drawing a Blank

It wasn't until the next morning that Sean finally managed to get someone to answer the phone at Sheridans. Every time he tried the landline it was engaged. Eventually though, on the ninth attempt, Niamh picked up.

'Probably Troy on the internet,' Niamh said when he complained. 'What's up?'

'You know that old place, Clifftop House?'

'I know where it is, yeah.'

'Well, I was talking to Grandad about it last night and he said that people used to use it for smuggling guns and stuff.'

'Wow!' Niamh replied. 'You know – I don't think I've ever actually been up there.'

'Anyway,' Sean went on, 'he said no one could live up there now because it's not safe. But I saw a light at the place.'

There was a pause before Niamh answered. 'You mean... from inside the house?'

'Yeah,' Sean said. 'It came on, stayed on for a few seconds, and then went off.'

'Sounds like it could be worth checking out, all right – you wanna come round so we can talk about it?'

'Sure. You wanna call Vinnie as well?'

'Nah, that's okay. He's already here.'

'What took you?' Niamh said when he finally got to Sheridans. 'Thought you said you'd be round early.'

'I had to go on a message for Mum,' Sean said. That, the long hike up to the Sheridans' mansion, plus knowing that the three of them were already there and planning something without him, made him sound tetchy. 'She wanted me to do more, but I said I was in a hurry.'

'Brave man,' Niamh replied. She knew Sean's Mum well.

'Stupid, you mean,' Sean said. 'Now I know what Grandad means when he says bravery and stupidity are pretty much the same thing.'

He followed Niamh into Matt's study, where Troy was messing around with the laptop.

'Come on, you, up. I need to check my e-mail,' Niamh said. She grabbed a handful of Troy's hair and threatened to lift him out of it. Literally.

'Sure. I'm finished.' Troy got up, pulled something off the printer and ran outside, muttering about being back in a minute.

'Well, whaddaya know – looks like Troy forgot to log out of his e-mail,' she said.

'What?'

'Didn't lock up,' Niamh said. She clicked on a

button marked 'Personal', and then on a second one marked 'Name'. A window opened with 'Outgoing Mail Name' on it and she rubbed out the words 'Troy' and 'Sheridan', then replaced them with the words 'Atomic' and 'Kitten' and logged him out.

'Any time he logs in to chat or send mail, it'll have that name on it,' she told him. 'Teach him to log off in future.'

She clicked around for a couple of minutes more and finally shook her head. 'Well, nothing new. Should have known really, considering I only checked it about ten minutes ago.' She logged off and shut down the computer. 'Come on then – everyone's out in the tree-house.'

'Everyone?'

'Well, Troy and Vinnie. We've been doing it up.'

'Doing it up' turned out to mean a major overhaul. The wooden walls were red and black, with pictures of a full-size Freddie Kruger, complete with steel fingers and dripping blood, painted all over. Troy's idea, Sean was willing to bet. He took one look at it and smiled – ah, the joys of being allowed to express yourself in paint.

'Hey, dude – what's up?' Vinnie asked. 'What did you find?'

'Well, you know that deserted old house up on the cliffs?' Sean said. 'Someone's apparently living there now. Even though it's supposed to be unsafe and about to fall apart.'

'Sean saw a light there,' added Niamh.

'A big mansion? Deserted? Lights? Oh, guys, we gotta go up there!'

'When?'

'Like… how about now?'

The house, at close quarters, looked like it had been blown up and then put back together again. Probably by Martians. It was three floors high and probably had had a fourth at some point. Vinnie looked up and took off the sunglasses. 'Mondo, dudes,' he said, half to himself. 'This is so cool.' He put the sunglasses back on again.

Sean looked at the house but failed to see how cool it was. One wrong step and there'd be a newspaper headline about four kids being trapped under a few tons of rubble. He looked across at the others but everyone else seemed to be on for a good explore.

'Hey… you think it's, like, haunted?' Vinnie asked.

'Who knows?' Sean said. 'Nine people died here – always possible.'

They had walked around to the front of the house where the hall door was boarded up. Vinnie, sunglasses still on, tried to pull one of the boards off, but it remained firm. 'Must be some other way in,' he said. 'Maybe we should look around the back or something?'

Troy stumbled through the long grass at the side. From a distance it looked as if a baseball cap was floating in mid air. 'We should come up here and offer to do the garden,' he called over. 'We'd make a fortune.'

'We could find a fortune, dudes,' Vinnie replied as he tried to rip the board off the front door again. 'This is not happening – this board's not moving for anything.'

Sean took a deep breath of relief. If they couldn't get in, they couldn't get hurt or get into trouble. Why did he have to go and tell them about the light in the first place? Suddenly he found himself wanting his nice peaceful boring summers.

Shut up, he reminded himself, you don't want that.

Suddenly Troy reappeared around the side of the house and called out, 'There's an entrance back here. I think we can get in.'

Oh, thanks a bunch, Troy!

One by one, they filed through a stone doorway that looked like it hadn't held a door in centuries. Inside, it was dark and dusty, with narrow splinters of sunlight shining in through cracks in the stone walls. Litter covered the floor and the only furniture was a large plank of wood held up by four empty crates to make a crude table on which lay a milk carton and a packet with a few slices of bread in it.

'Guess this was the kitchen,' Vinnie said.

'You don't say!' Sean murmured as he wandered away from the others. His eye fell on an old newspaper with a Garfield cartoon. He bent down to read it, then noticed something underneath it. He reached over, picked up a small notebook and flicked through the pages. There was writing on only two of the pages – a jumble of weird-looking codes and numbers.

'Wha'... wha're yous doin' back here again...?' a voice said suddenly.

Sean swallowed hard as a large pile of news-papers in one corner began to move.

'Niamh! Vinnie! Troy!' he tried to shout, but all that came out was a strangled croak.

Niamh rushed over. 'What is *that?*' she yelled.

Whatever it was sat up. Newspapers fell away on all sides. Then it turned and they all peered at the hairiest face any of them had ever seen in their lives. This thing made the guy from the Dubliners look like something from a Gillette commercial.

And 'it' was not very happy at having his afternoon nap interrupted.

'Who da hell d'yiz think y'are?' it shouted. '*Diss is MY gaff!!* I told yiz tha' before...'

'Eh, yes sir, sorry sir... we're just leaving, sir... man...' Vinnie hissed back. 'Come on, dudes! Run!'

The four of them piled back out into the sunny jungle outside and ploughed across what used to be the garden.

The tramp came after them, at least for a few steps, yelling something that none of them managed to catch. Then he grabbed a shopping trolley from somewhere and threw it across the garden after them. It travelled about three feet before it collapsed. Then he disappeared back inside.

'What was he on about?' Troy asked.

'Something about us not going back there again,' Sean told him. 'I think.'

'Well, at least we found something,' Niamh said, a glint of relief in her eyes. 'Someone really does live in there.'

The feeling of relief Sean felt at having escaped without being physically clobbered soon vanished. Instead, he began to feel like an idiot. He had dragging the Circle up to Clifftop House for nothing.

Vinnie had been insufferably patronising, saying that he shouldn't feel too bad and at least it was something to laugh about.

Sean, however, couldn't help feeling a bit

foolish. So much so that it wasn't until he was going to bed that he began to recall what had actually happened and notice something significant in what the tramp had said.

I told you never to come back *again* was what he'd said. He hadn't said it very clearly – in fact, he'd been even more incoherent that Grandad after a few drinks – but he had definitely used the word 'again'. Which meant someone else had been up there before them.

Question was, who? And was it worth telling the others? He decided no. There was no way he could go through the trauma of dragging everyone up there again – only to find out that tramp number one had been referring to a rival tramp or something even less interesting.

As he was taking off his jeans, he felt something hard in his pocket. He pulled out the notebook and stared at it as if he was wondering how it got there.

I must have put it there when that tramp woke up, he thought to himself. He leafed through it slowly, but the symbols and signs didn't make any sense. In the end he just put it away and went to bed.

He fell asleep having made a mental note to never, ever, mention Clifftop House again.

6 Sandstone Head

The following morning, when he went back to Sheridans, the whole thing seemed to have been forgotten about. Vinnie was lying on the wooden floor of the tree-house with a newspaper spread out in front of him while Niamh was reading a book of poetry by a guy called Shel Silverstein and giggling to herself. Troy was downstairs in the main house surfing the internet.

'Man, you do have a lot of crime in this place,' Vinnie said, as he turned the page. 'Seems like everyone's being robbed around here. There are three burglaries on this page alone. All in the same estate, too. Place called Sandstone Head.'

'That's the holiday development,' Sean told him. 'They had a lot of burglaries there last summer, too. The guards think it was a couple of guys from Montana Estate.'

'Maybe we could head down there and, like, maybe check it out?' Vinnie said.

'What do you think?' Sean asked Niamh.

Niamh just looked across at Vinnie and shrugged. In other words, they were going.

And so, an hour or so later, Niamh, Vinnie and

Sean sat under a tree in the woods behind the small row of the seven 'specially built state-of the-art luxury holiday residences' that was Sandstone Head. They had opted to stake out the back gardens because, they figured, it was much more likely that a burglar would try the back first.

Only three of the houses were actually occupied, but as soon as summer really kicked in all seven would be alive with families.

They had tried to drag Troy away from the computer screen, but he was too busy chatting to his internet girlfriend and spinning lies about how wonderful he was. At the moment, he was going for a cross between David Beckham and the guy from the Diet Coke advert.

'This could take a while,' Sean said, as he picked up a branch and started pulling the leaves off it. 'What are we looking for?'

'Anything unusual,' Vinnie replied. 'Kinda quiet at the moment, isn't it?'

Sean nodded privately. Maybe Troy had had the right idea after all.

They sat there for a good twenty minutes, waiting for something suspicious to happen, but the only thing they saw was a rather scraggy-looking cat that hissed before disappearing through a hole in a nearby fence. It was only when Sean was about to suggest that they give up and go home that Vinnie sat up suddenly and pointed at the house nearest to them.

'Hey!' he said suddenly. 'Over there!'

Sean and Niamh sat up. 'Where?'

'Beside the garage – someone's climbing up on to the garage. See?'

Sean put his hands up to his eyes to try and shield them from the sun and squinted. Sure enough, a figure was hauling itself up on the roof of the garage. Taller than they were and probably a bit older. He slipped and nearly fell back down, but managed to hold on to a pipe and scramble back up again.

'Dudes, I think we have our burglar,' Vinnie said. 'You think we should go in?'

'Someone should,' Niamh said, 'and someone should stay here and call the guards in case it gets nasty.'

'I'll go,' Sean said.

'You sure?' Vinnie said.

Sean nodded and took a deep breath. What choice did he have? If he didn't go, then Vinnie would go and he'd be even more insufferable than he already was.

'Way to go, dude! Just make sure you stay out of sight. You don't want him to see you, okay?'

Sean nodded. He took one last deep breath, sprinted across the clearing to the row of back gardens and slipped in through a gap in the fence.

The burglar was now up on the roof of the garage, trying to force the window open. Then he changed his mind and simply pushed it open – the morons who were renting the place hadn't even bothered to lock up! He looked around and climbed in, leaving the window open for a quick getaway.

Sean crept across the lawn, climbed up on to the garage roof as fast as he could, pulled himself up on to the window ledge and went in.

It suddenly occurred to him that he hadn't worked out what he had planned to do when he confronted the burglar. What could he do? Follow him around and see what he was taking? Memorise what he looked like and what he was wearing so that he could describe him accurately to the police? Make a citizen's arrest? And get a broken nose? No thanks! In fact, there had been no point at all in having followed him into the house.

For the hundredth time, he bemoaned the lack of a mobile. If he had one, he could have phoned Vinnie and Niamh, given them a running commentary on progress and gotten them to phone the police.

It was all Vinnie's fault. How could the stupid idiot have sent him off on such a wild goose chase The guy had sawdust between the ears.

He closed the window behind him. At least he

could stop the burglar from making that quick getaway.

He looked around the room. Suitcases on the bed, a pile of clothes thrown into a chair, a row of shoes along one side as if someone had been unpacking. Nothing there to interest a burglar. He went out on to the landing and peered over the banisters into the hall beneath.

Suddenly there was a clicking noise, like someone opening the front door. Sean froze, not even daring to breathe. Then he heard a voice with an English accent say, 'Mum, I got it open. We forgot to lock it when we went out, so I didn't have to force it or anything.'

'Great, Daniel,' a woman's voice answered. 'I thought we were going to have to ring the fire brigade or the police. I tried that wretched letting agent on my mobile but all I got was a message promising to ring back later.'

Sean felt himself breaking out in a cold sweat. Suddenly, the penny dropped with a loud clink – Daniel and his mother were obviously renting the place and had locked themselves out.

Time to make a quick and soundless exit.

He turned. His foot caught in a stupid little bamboo table that was lurking on the landing. A heavy pot with an enormous jungle plant crashed to the ground. He could feel rather than see Daniel and Mum stopping in their tracks.

'Burglars!' shouted Mum.

Burglars? Sean thought, horribly. Only now did he realise that if he got caught, the police would probably pin not only this but every other burglary at Sandstone Head over the last two years on him.

Then heavy footsteps sounded on the stairs. Daniel was coming back up!

Sean dashed into the bedroom, opened the window with an effort (what a brilliant idea closing it had been!) and got out on to the garage roof. He lowered himself to the ground and ran like hell. Just as Mum came around the side of the house with a broom, screaming, 'Stop! Thief!' at the top of her voice.

Luckily, Daniel was in such a hurry to get down that he missed his footing on the roof and stumbled as he landed. Sean made the most of this godsend and was soon squeezing back through the fence.

'Move!' he yelled at the others.

'What happened?'

'Tell you later – come on!'

They grabbed their bikes and cycled down the main road toward the beach, separating at the junction. Sean took the road home, bending low over the handlebars as a police car passed.

It was headed for Sandstone Head.

7 Bach and Biscuits

Most of Mum's friends had turned up for the Bach and Biscuits recital next morning by the time the postman arrived with some bills and a glossy postcard with a picture of sun-baked London on it for Sean. He legged it upstairs to read it.

How R U?
Having fun in London – got lost on the tube 3 times (twice deliberately!) and managed to punch 1 of those guard soldier-guard-thingy-guys in the stomach. Going 2 a haunted castle 2nite, so sme1 had better warn the ghost! Glad UR not here J,

Cara

PS Dad sez hi.

Sean pinned the postcard to the wall above his bed and went back downstairs, where the circle were ploughing through the coffee and short-bread fingers Mum had spent most of yesterday making. At least it had kept her busy. Now, though, they were vanishing like cigarettes in a teachers' staff-room.

'Did you hear about the break-in yesterday at

Sandstone Head' said a woman in a large green hat suddenly.

Sean's ears pricked up instantly.

'I did,' replied the woman sitting beside her. 'And it's not the first from what I hear – there have been a few. Why, my sister's husband's employee's nephew was here last week and they were hit. Not that they had anything valuable to steal – but it's the principle of the thing.'

There was a big *oooh* and Green Hat visibly shivered. 'It's a crime wave. And nobody's safe until they do something about it.'

Confirmation of the crime wave arrived a few minutes later when a woman in a long flowing cape that Superman would have been proud of arrived with the local rag in her hand. There was a headline on the back page:

Burglary attempt at Sandstone Head.
Intruders foiled by
bravery of holidaymakers.

She read on: 'Yesterday afternoon, a daring attempt was made by a gang of youths to burgle one of the holiday homes at Sandstone Head. Only for the courage of Mrs Higginbottom and her son, Daniel, there is no doubt but that their house would have been ransacked and their valuables would have disappeared. Daniel almost caught the intruder, whom he described as a small weedy youth with pimples...'

A small weedy youth with pimples...? Sean nearly choked.

'Unfortunately, just as Daniel was about to grab the leader, he tripped over an obstacle which had been placed in his path by one of the gang. Garda Fitzgerald said that the police viewed the attempted break-in very seriously and would leave no stone unturned in their attempts to apprehend the perpetrators of this crime which strikes at the very foundations of our state...'

'Is this the welcome we show our valuable tourists?' Visible indignation from an old dear in the corner. 'Why, if we carry on like that, we won't have any in the future.'

Sean sat listening. No wonder Grandad said you could never trust what you read in the papers. He had already been turned into a pimple-faced nerd and a gang had been conjured up out of thin air. But had anyone actually seen anything? The Bach and Biscuits set were always wandering around, walking their dogs and spying on people.

'Are the police anywhere near to finding the criminals?' he asked, carefully.

'You must be joking,' replied Green Hat. 'The police are doing just what they normally do with everything. *Nothing.*'

'They say it's an out-of-town gang,' quavered a wrinkly old dear with a stick.

'Nonsense!' Green Hat cut her short. 'That's what they always say. Can't be bothered looking for clues that are right under their noses. But I like to think *I* know who's behind it...'

Here we go, Sean thought, sitting down at the piano and trying to look innocent. Round up the usual suspects.

'...those Sheridan brats. And probably that young Ryan one as well.'

Sean relaxed. Once people started talking about Troy and Niamh, he knew they hadn't a clue. If they had, they'd be down at the police station creating hell for whoever was behind the desk.

Mum gently steered everyone to the front room while Grandad took the opportunity to make a quick exit.

For the next forty minutes or so, Sean simply switched to autopilot and rattled off whatever it was they wanted him to rattle off, throwing in a spirited version of *Top Hat* at the end. This brought a muted murmur from Green Hat in the corner.

'Dear boy, you'll *ruin* your style, playing all that awful... jazz,' she said. 'No, you really can't argue with the classics.'

Sean stood up and while Mum was acknowledging the nodding and applause he slipped out like a scalded cat.

Like Grandad, like grandson.

When he got round to Sheridans, he gave them a full rundown of the rumours that were circulating. The gospel according, mainly, to Green Hat.

'Well, at least nobody identified you,' consoled Niamh.

'And they'll be out looking for a gang,' Troy added.

'We *are* a gang,' Sean pointed out.

Trust Troy to think of something designed to set the nerves jangling. Just when he was beginning to feel safe.

'Don't like to say it, dude, but it looks like you blew it.'

'*What?*' Sean wanted to punch the smugly smiling face.

'You lost the plot, man! Here's what you should have done. That time you were standing on the landing, when they were down in the hall, that was the time for cool thinking. You should have gone down the stairs, told them that you were part of Neighbourhood Watch, that you'd seen someone breaking and entering and that, disregarding all thought of danger, you'd followed him into the house with the intention of clocking him and reporting the matter to the police. Then you would have been hailed as a hero instead of being fingered as a burglar.'

'I didn't intend to get fingered at all,' said Sean

between his teeth. 'My plan was to make a clean getaway.'

'Well you didn't, did you?'

'Have you heard about Kerr?' Niamh jumped in a little too quickly.

'No?'

'He's been thrown out of the safari game show!'

The vote had been eleven to one and Kerr would be on the next plane home. Every single one of Kerr's rivals had said the same thing; they didn't like 'Joseph' because he was too sarcastic and treated them like children.

'I still think he treated them better than us,' Niamh mused. 'I can't believe he got voted off. I thought he'd be sure to stay on when that woman messed up the lion-catching challenge and they had to forfeit half their food.'

'Have we got nothing better to talk about than Kerr?' Troy said. 'What about the smuggling?'

'Yeah, while you being musical,' Vinnie explained to Sean, 'we were doing some research. Didn't you hear about the drugs bust yesterday?'

'But that was in the midlands,' Sean said. 'We're nowhere near the midlands.'

'Well, that stuff has to come in somewhere, by air or sea – why not here?'

'But it's just so... unlikely,' objected Sean. He tried to see Five Rivers – dull, sleepy, unexciting Fiver Rivers – as the drug-smuggling epicentre of the country and failed.

'But there *was* something going on at Clifftop House,' said Niamh. 'You saw the lights and Vinnie saw them too.'

'He did?'

'Yeah, when I was walking my cousin's dog I just happened to look up at the house and guess what? Lights! Real flashing lights, dude – just like the one you saw. Seemed to be a pattern to them.'

Suddenly, Sean felt vindicated. So something *was* going on up there – it wasn't just a tramp using it as a kip.

'I think we should go up there again, dudes,' said Vinnie. 'Like... tonight. See if we can find out what's happening and who's making those lights. And why.'

'Are you serious?' Sean said. 'If there are smugglers there, it could be dangerous.'

'We're only going to have a look,' argued Niamh. 'We're not going to confront anyone.'

'We can say that we were ghost hunting or something,' said Troy. 'That we'd heard that the place was haunted and were just checking it out. We'd get away with it.'

'So it's settled then, dudes. All we need to do now is set a time!'

I cannot believe we're doing this, thought Sean. Are we actually going to go up to that scary old house and check it out for smugglers? That

Vinnie is three sheets in the wind. Still, if we find nothing, maybe they'll drop the idea and that will be all to the good.

On the other hand, he told himself later, wasn't this the sort of thing I wanted to be involved in less than a week ago?

8 The Secret Steps

That night, Sean went to bed a bit earlier, hoping to get some sleep before eleven, but it was hopeless. He was far too wound up. Every time he closed his eyes, images of being chased by smugglers flashed before him.

The clock slowly ticked its way round to half ten and Sean reached out and switched off the alarm, long before it was due to go off. He got out of bed, dressed again, and stepped out of his window on to the garage roof. From there it was a simple jump down on to the driveway, then out of the estate and up towards Clifftop House. He wasn't surprised to discover that he was the last to get there, but he didn't mind that. Better than being the first.

'Yo dude, how's it hanging?' Vinnie said. He still had the sunglasses on.

'Em... fine, I think...'

The house itself looked even creepier at night than during the day. That worrying about-to-fall-over look hadn't gone away, but now it had been joined by a how-am-I-still-standing? look.

Everything was silent. No sounds, nothing.

After a cautionary wait, Vinnie led them into

the house by the back entrance. Inside, it was so dark that they might as well have had their eyes closed. It was going to make it difficult to see, never mind find, anything.

'I can't see a thing,' Sean muttered. 'We should have brought a...'

He was cut off by a beam of light coming from behind him. It was bright enough to light up a medium-sized planet. He made the mistake of looking around and staring right into the beam. It nearly blinded him. He ducked out of the way, crashed into a large box and fell over. He stayed down until he managed to scrape most of the light out of his eyes. 'Hey! What's happening?'

'Wow, sorry dude – didn't know you standing right in front of me,' said Vinnie. He didn't sound a bit, though, Sean seethed. Bet he did it on purpose.

'Where did you get *that?*' Troy asked. 'And where can I get one?'

'Mondo torch I picked up in the States. Cost over a hundred bucks.'

'So, cheaper than the sunglasses, eh?' Sean said.

'Price of being cool, dude.'

Didn't know you could buy cool, Sean thought, as he slowly got back to his feet. He blinked a few times and peered at the faces in front of him. Troy was laughing, the other two looked as if they thought he was a prat.

'Well, at least we know for certain there's no one around,' Niamh said. 'That crash would have woken up anything.'

'Okay, dudes, let's split up. Niamh and I can check one of the front rooms, you guys have a look at the other.'

'For what?' Troy sounded fed up.

The light wasn't much stronger in the front rooms. Sean wished he had the torch which Vinnie was flashing around in the other room. Not that there was much to see – the entire room was empty of everything but dust.

'Nobody in here,' said Sean, with a complete sense of relief. 'Not even that tramp.'

'Or whoever is flashing the lights,' Troy replied.

Niamh and Vinnie mustn't have found anything either because they had gone back into the kitchen. Sean decided to join and suggest that they get home *now!*

Back in the main hall with its boarded-up front door, he noticed a small door under the stairs. He pushed it back very slowly, almost afraid that the stairs might crash down. It creaked loudly. Beyond it there was nothing but a few ghostly steps leading down to darkness. What was down there? A basement, maybe? If it was, then he really didn't want to know about it.

Better shut the door again quickly before the others see it or they'll want to go down and find out where it leads, he decided. And I don't, thank you very much.

Suddenly there was a crash, followed by a scream. Either Vinnie or Troy. There was the sound of heavy footsteps – too heavy to be any of them. Someone must have come in. In fact, more than one.

He turned and opened the door under the stairs. He could stay there until everything was quiet. But as he stepped down on to the first step, it gave way and he slipped backwards. He reached out for a rail or something to grab, but his flailing hands found nothing. His jacket caught on a projecting bit of wall, but it was not strong enough to hold him. There was a loud ripping noise as it tore and Sean fell backwards, ending up on a small landing where the steps turned.

Slowly, he picked himself up. His knee hurt where he'd banged it off a wall, but it wasn't serious – at least he could stand up. But now what? In the darkness, he felt cool air blowing on his face. It was coming from below. These steps must lead outside somewhere, he reasoned. I can get out this way.

He reached out, felt the wall opposite and made his way carefully down the steps. As he went down, the light began to get stronger. Eventually, he came to a large platform.

Where the hell am I? he wondered. He stepped

down on to what felt like... *sand?*

It *was* sand! The floor of a cave – one of the many that riddled the coastline. He walked to the end and came out on to bare sands. On his left was the main beach and on the right was the cove and the old disused boathouse that seemed to belong to no one.

But this was no time for taking bearings, this was time for action. If those intruders were smugglers, what was happening? Had they fallen for the story about ghost-hunting? Where were Niamh, Troy and Vinnie?

The police – he had to get to the police and tell them what was going on!

He sprinted off up to the Coast Road. By the time he got there, his lungs were burning but he didn't dare stop. He set off for the shopping centre and the police station across the road, getting there just as a police car pulled into the yard. It stopped and a door opened.

He nearly fell backwards when he saw Niamh, Troy and Vinnie step out.

He ducked down behind some bushes. What was going on? Had the police been at the house? Why? Who were the owners of those heavy footsteps he had heard? The police – or the smugglers? If indeed, there were any smugglers...

One of the guards looked across the road as he got out of the car and Sean dipped his head under the bushes. But the guard just yawned and followed the others into the brightly lit police station.

There didn't seem to be much point in either hanging around or going into the police station. Sean backed away and sneaked off back down the road before someone saw him and started asking even more awkward questions.

9 Grounded

By the time Sean climbed over the fence and staggered up the back garden to the house it was beginning to get bright again. He was going to be very happy when he was back in his nice warm bed because he was wrecked.

He hauled himself up on to the garage and quietly pulled his window open. The only noise that filled the air was that of Grandad snoring in the next room.

He stepped into the room, pulled the window shut and took a deep breath. Finally, he was safe.

'Where in God's name have you been?'

He nearly went through the roof.

Somehow, he managed to turn around and face his mother. 'Em… I woke up early and I just nipped out for a walk,' he said hopefully. Even as the words left his mouth, he knew it wasn't going to work. There were more holes in his story than a pair of Troy's socks, but he couldn't even think of anything else to say.

'You were out with those Sheridans, weren't you?' said Mum. It was not a question. It was a statement

Sean opened his mouth to say 'No', but Mum

hissed, 'Don't argue with me! I was frantic with worry – I was almost going to call the police. I thought you'd run away.'

Oh, dear God, don't start that... I am not in the mood for this.

'Sean, I have asked you again and again and again to stay away from those spoiled little monsters and time and time again you have refused.'

'But they're the only friends I've got. We just... wanted to watch the sunrise, that's all.'

He thought, where the hell did that one come from? It was the best excuse he'd ever come up with! Talk about pressure bringing out the best in you – he might just pull this one out of the fire yet.

Mum pursed her lips. 'I'm sorry, Sean, but you leave me with no choice.'

On the other hand, he might not.

'I can't have them getting you to sneak out in the middle of the night, up to God knows what, and then lying to me when you come back,' Mum went on. 'I'm sending you up to your Aunt Muriel's in Dundalk for the rest of the summer.'

'*What?*'

'That way, you won't be under the influence of a couple of common criminals.'

'They're not criminals.' Whatever happened, that one point needed to be made. 'They're just...

different… creative… fun…'

'Well I don't like them. They are a bad influence. I've told you to keep away from them; now I'll have to take *you* away from them. I'll ring Muriel in the morning and see if she can pick you up in the afternoon.'

'But you can't!'

She walked past him and went out with the words, 'Now get some sleep. And you're not to leave the house again until Aunt Muriel gets here. Is that clear?'

'Yes, Mum.'

Next door, Grandad was still snoring. Why hadn't he come in and told Mum how unreasonable she was? She had talked loudly enough to wake him up. Last time he'll get me to play Scrabble with him.

Sean's alarm clock went off at the normal time the next morning but he just rolled over and closed his eyes. Not only was he exhausted after last night's adventures, but he figured ducking the routine didn't matter anyway. He couldn't get *two* summers in Dundalk.

He got up for lunch, which was eaten in dead silence. No one spoke a single word until Mum got up from the table and said, 'I have to go out for a short while – Denise has had another argument with John and needs calming down.'

That was good news. Denise lived on the far side of the town.

'Now you are still grounded,' she continued. 'I suggest you use the time to get some piano practice in and don't even think of giving me that look. I'm not in the mood for it. Grandad will make sure you stay in – he's in charge.'

When she left, Sean gave her ten minutes before making for the front door.

'I thought you were supposed to be grounded,' said Grandad appearing out of nowhere.

Sean stopped for a second and stared at him. 'I'm just going to Niamh and Troy's.

'You know I can be bribed,' Grandad went on.

'Large bag of wine gums?'

Grandad smiled his trademark toothless smile. 'If she phones, I'll say you're in the shower. If she gets back early, deal's off. You're on your own.'

'Thanks, Grandad.'

There are times when it's downright stupid not to take a chance, he figured. What was the worst Mum could do to him now? Send him even further that Dundalk? Ground him for longer?

Matt was mowing the front lawn as he cycled up. He dropped his bike at the front of the house and stuck his head round the hall door where Olwyn was talking on the phone.

'Oh hello, Sean,' she said looking up. 'They're still in bed, if you want to go up?'

'If it's okay…?'

'Of course it is! You're practically part of the family.'

He ran up the stairs and banged on Niamh's door.

'Who is it?' she called.

'Me, Sean.'

'I'm just getting up – see you in Troy's room in a few minutes.'

He banged on Troy's door and went in. Troy was still in bed and Vinnie was asleep on a mattress on the floor. He was still wearing the sunglasses.

'What're you doing so here so early?'

'It's ten to two!' Sean replied. He couldn't help feeling a bit… well… hurt at not being invited to sleepover. Even though he probably wouldn't have been allowed.

'It is?' Troy put his head back down on the pillow. 'Call me at five.'

Niamh came in and poked Vinnie awake. 'And where did you get to last night?'

'I found a secret passage-way and fell down it,' Sean told them as casually as he could. 'Didn't lead anywhere, just down to a cave and out on to the beach. It's probably been there since the gun-running. How did you guys wind up in the police station?'

'The police busted us,' Vinnie said. 'Three of

them with batons. Said they'd seen lights. What I'd like to know is why they were up at Clifftop House themselves.'

'They asked us what we were doing there,' Niamh said. 'We trotted out the looking-for-ghosts story but I don't think they really bought it, so they took us down to the police station.'

'Asked us loads of questions,' Troy put in.

'I think they thought we were forging bank-notes or passports, or something like that. As if! Anyway, they phoned Matt and Olwyn, who came down and picked us up.'

'What did they say?' asked Sean.

'Nothing – they believe in ghosts. To a point, anyway.'

Not for the first time, Sean felt a burning jealousy. Why couldn't he have had parents like that? 'You didn't tell them about the smugglers, then?'

'Nope. I think we might have gotten it wrong there, anyway. Those lights were probably just the tramp's torch or candle or something. I'm beginning to think you were right – this place is a dead-end. We must have been mad to think smugglers would pick it.'

But that's exactly why smugglers would pick it, Sean thought. There's a big bay for ships, lots of people coming and going in the summer, a house no one ever goes near – it's ideal.

'So you got back safely, then?' Troy said.

'Not exactly – I got caught coming in.'

It was Niamh's turn to be surprised. 'You're kidding? How? What happened?'

'I don't know,' Sean said, sitting down on the end of Troy's bed. He hadn't actually asked himself that question, not that it mattered. Maybe Mum, in a wild fit of fantasy, had concluded that they were behind the 'break-in' at Sandstone Head and probably other places as well. All circumstantial of course, but then Human Rights didn't extend to children with parents. 'Anyway I'm grounded and she's sending me up to Dundalk later this evening. I usually go there for a couple of weeks holiday in August.'

'And now you're being sent there for getting into trouble,' Niamh said. 'Hope you don't mind me saying this, but your mother is weird.'

'No... not at all.'

'You want me to talk to her for you, dude?' Vinnie said without moving. Sean could have sworn he was asleep. 'I can sweet-talk her round to let you stay, man. Say you're sorry, take the flack, that sort of thing.'

'You'll never do it,' Sean said. 'Anyway I'll try and get back sooner rather than later. If I can get round Aunt Muriel, that is.'

'No problemo, man. Your call.'

'Listen, I'm going to have to run – I'm not

supposed to have left the house,' Sean said.

The others nodded understandingly as Sean headed off, trying not to think of the possibility of not seeing them again for a couple of months.

He got back with ten minutes to spare before Mum pulled into the driveway and just hung around watching TV until Aunt Muriel arrived later that evening.

It was only on the way up to Dundalk in the twilight that he realised what he was leaving behind. The summer he so wanted had been taken away, given back, and now was being taken away again. Even Vinnie, underneath all the 'dudes', the 'mans' and the sunglasses, was not such a prat. He was going to miss him, too. If he had time, he could probably really get to like the guy and be friends with him. But he didn't have time. Mum had seen to that. He was going away and they would be doing all the things he'd wanted to do. Sleepovers, weekends away, the whole bag of wine gums.

That was when he made the decision.

No way am I staying up there. No way. I've got to find a way back and I've got to make Mum see that it's not fair to make me spend the summer away from my friends.

I'm going back.

10 Ruud to the Rescue

A horrible screeching noise woke him the next morning. He sat up, whacked his head off something and sat back clutching it. 'Ow... what in sod's name was that?'

Outside, whatever it was screeched again. Now that he was a bit more awake, he recognised it as a cockerel. *The* cockerel. The mother of all cock-rels. Rodney.

Oh, yes, Dundalk. It all came back to him.

He swore to himself and tried to get back to sleep, but it was impossible. He was awake now. In the end he got up and started unpacking out of sheer boredom. He had a habit of packing forty odd t-shirts and two pairs of underpants for trips to Aunt Muriel's, though this time he seemed to have gotten enough of everything. He dug his fingers under a pair of jeans and they ran into what felt like a book.

He frowned as he pulled it out. It was the notebook he'd found at Clifftop House, the first time they'd gone up there. He kicked himself. He should really have given it to the others before he left – it was no use to him here. But was it any use to anyone? If there were no smugglers then what was it? The hairy tramp's laundry list written in Sanskrit?

Well, he couldn't do anything about it now. He threw it back into the suitcase and went downstairs to see if anyone else was up.

Before he even got to the bottom of the stairs, he heard a tapping sound, as if someone was typing away on a computer. But Aunt Muriel didn't have one. He pushed open the kitchen door to see his cousin, Steffi, sitting at the table and typing away on a laptop. He couldn't help noticing how much she'd changed since he saw her last. She was slimmer and much more attractive than the spotty little twerp he'd seen last Christmas. It was amazing what a difference six months made.

'Morning,' he said.

'Oh, hiya,' Steffi said, looking up. 'You made it up okay, then?'

Sean nodded. 'Nice machine,' he said.

'It's Dad's. Five twelve megabyte ram, sixty-four gigabyte hard drive, DVD player and CD-ROM, even a built-in 250meg zip-drive,' Steffi said. 'Not bad.'

Sean took her word for it. He pulled out a packet of cereal and made himself some breakfast.

'So why are you here?' she asked bluntly. 'You're not usually dragged up until August.'

'I'm not sure,' Sean told. 'I'm either here as a punishment or on holiday.'

'I can see how that would be confusing...'

Sean smiled and explained everything that had happened. It didn't really make things any clearer to him, but Steffi seemed to understand. Maybe she could explain it to him some day?

'So, what is there to do around here?' he asked.

'Exactly the same as there was last year. And the year before that. And the year before that, too. Want me to go on?'

Sean shook his head. How did she handle the excitement? he wondered as he sat down at the table.

He had to get out of here. There was no way he was going to be able to stick more than a day in this place at the most. Last year it had been different. The Daredevils had changed all that.

'How do you get out of here? To Dundalk for a start?'

'Bus-stop's a mile away,' Steffi said, 'but the next bus isn't until twenty-five past seven. Then they come every two-and-a-half-hours. Bus fare's one euro twenty.'

One euro twenty. And train ticket on top of that. Plus bus fare back to Five Rivers. And where would he stay once he got back there? He'd have to contact the others beforehand. Somehow. The nearest phone was... well, it wasn't close by .

Then another thought hit him. Next bus was when? Seven something...?

'Eh, Steffi? What time is it now...?'

'Six-seventeen.'

'Six *what?* You're kidding?'

'Nope,' Steffi sniggered. 'Better get used to it.'

To fill in the time until the next meal was due, he told her about Clifftop House, the tramp, the suspected smugglers and nearly getting arrested for Breaking and Entering. When he came to the bit about the notebook, Steffi pricked up her ears. 'A notebook? What was in it?'

'Some sort of code – I couldn't read it.'

'Do you still have it? Show it to me...'

Sean raced upstairs and got the notebook. She frowned as she looked at the two pages of squiggles and figures. 'This isn't code, you stupid thick,' she said. 'It's a foreign language. One of the Scandinavian ones maybe... or Dutch...' She shook her head. 'No, definitely Dutch.'

'Can you read it?'

'No, but I might know someone who can...'

Stephanie clicked on a few icons and brought up two new windows on the computer screen. Finally, she brought up an e-mail page. Sean recognized it from Niamh and Troy's computer. 'I know a guy in Holland that I chat with sometimes. He's not online at the moment, but I can send him an e-mail with the pages. He should be able to translate them.'

'You're connected to the internet?' Sean said. 'I thought you didn't have a phone?'

'We don't. We have a phone line we don't use, though, so we can connect through that. Now let's see… Ruud…'

She scanned the notes into the computer so that exact replicas of the pages were stored as files in her computer. Then she simply attached copies of the scans to an e-mail and sent it off. In five minutes it was all over and the contents of the notebook were now sitting in Ruud's inbox in Holland, waiting for him to have a look and write back.

'So what now?' Sean said.

'We wait. Could be a few hours, though.'

They spent most of the rest of the morning feeding animals and cleaning up after them. Sean didn't mind helping out around the farm. It was better than sitting around doing nothing and it did take his mind off things – once he got used to the smell. Steffi, on the other hand, disappeared very quickly. The entire family seemed to make a habit of it. Aunt Muriel was inside making cakes for some meeting that she was hosting and he hadn't even seen Uncle Pat yet.

When Sean came in for lunch, he found Steffi messing about on the laptop again.

'Where did you get to?' Sean asked. 'I thought you were supposed to be helping me?'

'Checking my e-mail,' Steffi replied.

'Any word from Ruud?'

'Not yet. Probably be out all day.'

'What are the plans for the afternoon?' Sean said. 'I only work half days. Child Labour Laws.'

'Could go into Dundalk, if you want. There are a couple of good films on. I won't be here tomorrow, I'm going to Dublin with my friend Jenny.'

Sean perked up. 'Dublin?'

'Yeah. We're going to a gig. Hot-Lads,' Steffi told him, typing something into the computer.

'That overrated boy band? Are you mad?'

'I'm not pushed about them. I'm only going because Jenny bought me a ticket. And keep your voice down – Mum just thinks we're visiting her cousin in Dublin. She doesn't care for boy bands either.'

Oh, thanks, Sean thought. Put me and the disapproving parent in the same boat. Pity it's tomorrow, though. I can hardly reappear in Five Rivers only two days after I left. Why couldn't it have been next week?

'So what are you doing at the moment?'

'Chatting. Guy from South Africa who thinks he was abducted by aliens once. Bit of a prat, really.'

'You know a guy from South Africa?'

'I know people all over the world. Japan, France, Brazil, Ballydehob...'

'They have the internet in Ballydehob?'

'In remotest West Cork, yes,' Steffi said. 'Everywhere except Redmonds, Five Rivers.' She sat back and put on a thoughtful look. 'That's the internet for you: I chat with Anton from South Africa four or five times a week and I don't know when I last spoke to you or Aunt Veronica. Might as well be living on a different planet.'

Just then, the computer bleeped. 'Hello, I have a new e-mail from... Ruud! Yes! We have contact!'

A window with Ruud's name came up on the screen and an e-mail began to download with his name and e-mail address, followed by Stephanie's e-mail address, followed by the words, 'Subject: Notebook'

Hi Steffi! (it read) Got your notes for translation. They don't make much sense to me. They look like jottings. There's a list of numbers from 1 to 30. Opposite each is a three or four digit figure – 9.45, 10.38 and so on – could they be times? Some names are given – 'Ocean Warrior' and 'Sea Horse 2'. Ships? Then there is a sequence of dots and dashes, long and short and so on. I think this is some sort of code. Could it refer to lights.

Steffi printed it out and Sean took it off the printer.

'Sorry. I thought we were on to something there,' said Steffi, 'but it doesn't look very useful. Probably just the tramp taking down the names of passing ships for some reason. Doesn't explain the lights though.'

Sean didn't hear her. He was too busy studying the list Ruud had assumed to be times. 20.30, 21.12, 21.53, 22.40, 23.23.

Was there a kind of pattern to them? Each one was an advance on the previous figure. Always later.

Now what was an hour or thereabouts later every day.

Tides! How could he have forgotten? He thought back to the evening he and Niamh had been frantically checking tide times before going to rescue Troy.

He looked at the list again. Some of the figures were marked with an X. Usually the ones between ten at night and five in the morning. Could those be tides at night? That made sense. Who would want to be smuggling something in broad daylight?

He looked at the numbers from one to thirty. Days of the month? A few had a tiny circle over them. One was the number 17. Reading across the page he got:

17   22.40

The 22.40 was also marked.

'What date is it today?' he asked Steffi.

'Sunday, 16th of June,' she replied. 'Why?'

'Something is going to happen tomorrow night,' he told her excitedly. 'Look at the list. The 17th is marked and there's a high tide at 22.40.'

'What on earth are you talking about?' Steffi had that have-you-lost-it? look on her face.

'I've worked it out. One of the lists of figures is tides. High tides. The ones at night. The figures marked with the circle must be the days on which they're bringing in the drugs. Don't you see?'

Steffi still looked blank.

'We know there's a signal system from the boat to Clifftop House. But the drugs have to be landed at high tide when the water comes right up to the cliffs and into the cave. They're not going to land them on bare sand in a low tide, are they?

'So the guys at this end know the date and the approximate times a cargo is going to arrive. When the boat comes into the bay, approaching the time of high tide, signals are exchanged, a small boat is lowered and the drugs are run into the cave below. Then they're unloaded, taken up the steps I discovered, packed into the van and driven away to wherever they're supposed to go. Sometimes they're caught – like the guys in the midlands.'

Steffi's face broke into a big smile. 'Sean, you could be right... aren't you a genius... now what do we do? Alert the police?'

'You sure? I mean... will they really buy that? I mean, basically, all we have are a few figures. They could mean anything.'

For a second, he thought she was going to argue with him but surprisingly she didn't. She turned back to the laptop.

'I think the first thing we do is alert the Circle. What's Niamh's number?'

11 Chat Line

'What do you mean you can't remember Niamh's mobile number?' Steffi had stopped typing and was looking at him. 'How can I send her a text message when you don't know her number?'

Sean racked his brains. Six-six-seven something… or was it six-seven-seven…? Argh! Why couldn't he remember it?

Faced with an impatient Steffi, he tried to defend himself. 'Can't you send one without it? Even from the internet?'

'I still have to know the number – how else will it know where to go?'

All right, all right, so don't rub it in, Sean thought. I feel thick enough as it is.

But he'd have plenty of time to feel thick later – right now they had to get word of what might be about to happen in Five Rivers.

'Hang on,' Steffi said sitting back up, 'I've just had an idea… here we are… Five Rivers.'

Sean leaned over to see what she was talking about. On the screen a page from the internet was pulled up on one side with what looked like a list of names on the other. Mostly black with a few in red.

'Those are the names of people I chat with regularly when I'm online,' Steffi told him, pointing at the list of names. 'The ones in red are online right now, so we can talk to them. The ones in black are out. Only about forty of them are in Dublin, though. Now, who's in Five Rivers? KAT... no, he's in America at the moment. Bit of a prat anyway. Max83... too weird – worse than me. Ah, Casey90 – no, maybe not. Atomic Kitten... why's he suddenly calling himself Atomic Kitten?'

Suddenly Sean woke up. 'Atomic Kitten!'

'Yeah... you know him?'

'Sure! Niamh changed his name when he wasn't watching.'

Steffi's face lit up like O'Connell Street on Christmas Eve. 'You know Troy?'

'He's my friend. You... chat with him?'

'Yeah! He's such a dream!'

'He's *what?*'

'Hang on, I'll just send him a chat-message.' She typed away for a second and then said, 'He e-mailed me his picture. Look at this.' She spun round and brought up a picture on the screen. It was a muscular, blond, well-tanned teenager, a few years older than Sean. This guy had spent most of his life in the gym, though.

Sean couldn't help laughing.

'Steffi, I have news for you... that's not Troy.'

'It's... not?' For a few seconds she said nothing. Finally she took a deep breath. 'The little...'

They were interrupted by a message which had appeared on the screen all by itself: *Hey, babe whazzzup?*. It was from 'Atomic Kitten'.

'Did Troy just send you that?'

'Yep,' Steffi nodded. She turned back to the screen, and typed in a message: *Hi, Troy... how's life? Guess what! I'm coming to Dublin!* She brought the pointer on the screen up to a small box marked Send and clicked on it. 'Time for a little bit of fun with "Troy",' she said. 'And anyway, I am going to Dublin. The gig at the Meethook.'

A minute or so later, there was another bleep from the machine and some words appeared underneath Steffi's message. It was Troy's reply: *Really? Cool! We must meet up this time!*

'He always says that,' Steffi said. 'Then he either can't meet or gets sick or has to go on holiday or something. Now I know why.'

She typed in: *Yeah. I might bring my cousin, if that's OK with U?*

Another bleep: *Sure – what's her name?*

HIS name! And he's here on holiday. He actually lives in Dublin. In Five Rivers! She waited a second. 'Now to drop the H-bomb...': *He got sent up here by his Mum bcoz she thought he was breaking N2 some1's house.*

There was a long wait before the reply. At one

point Sean though he'd switched his computer off, but that wouldn't be like Troy. Finally, the reply appeared on the screen: *What's his name?*

This time it was Sean who wrote back: *It's me U dopey sod!! Sean! I'm her cousin!*

For a while, there was nothing. Then a reply came through that simply said, '*brb*'.

'"Be right back",' Stephanie translated. 'You chicken, Troy!'

Sean typed in another message: *And I found out what the codes in the copybook mean.*

U did? U rock, man! What R they?

That must be Vinnie, Sean thought: *The message isn't in code – the words are in Dutch. We had it translated and I think I've worked out what the figures are. Whatever's happening, I think it's going to happen tomorrow night!*

There was a pause before a reply came back: *Are you sure?*

Sean repeated: *Something is happening tomorrow night.*

There was another long pause. 'Is he still there?' Sean asked.

'He's still online,' Stephanie said, tapping the screen. 'If he goes off, his name will turn black.'

Sure enough there was a bleep on the screen and then a window opened on its own: *I was just getting Niamh and Troy back, dude. They can't wait 2 go up there again!*

'They'll get us all killed one of these days,' groaned Sean. He typed: *We could be talking criminals here!! For sod's sake, stay away from the thing and tell the police.*

Seconds later, the reply came back: *We'll be OK as long as we all go up there together. Don't worry – we'll tell Matt.*

Tell him what? If Matt hears a mention of 'drug smugglers' he'll tell them exactly the same thing I just did.

Steffi pulled the computer away from Sean and typed something as fast as she could. Then she sat back smiling and switched off the machine.

'What was that all about?' Sean hadn't been able to see what she was writing. 'I was enjoying that.'

'I had to send a private message. You wouldn't have liked it.'

'Why? What did you say?'

Steffi sat back in her chair with an embarrassed grin on her face. Whatever she had done, Sean was sure that he wasn't going to like it. In fact, he had the feeling he was going to freak out when he heard it.

'I told them not to do anything tomorrow night...' Steffi told him.

Relief flooded over him

'... until we got down there.'

12 To the Meethook

Sean woke up the next morning without Rodney blasting him out of it. He sat up slowly and wondered what had happened to the poor thing. Heart attack? Then he had a horrible thought.

He looked over at the clock: 6:04.

Oh wonderful, he thought. I'm falling asleep at ten and waking up at six. This is really going to stuff up my sleeping patterns.

He rolled over and tried to get back to sleep. He was just drifting off when Rodney let rip. At that point, he got up and went downstairs. Some fights you just cannot win.

Steffi and he spent the rest of the day feeding animals, looking bored, and trying not to give the game away. At about four, they grabbed their things and headed over to Jenny's place. Jenny turned out to be sixteen and had even gone to the trouble of getting Sean an extra ticket.

'I hope no one ever finds out that someone bought me a ticket for Hot-Lads,' Sean said.

'Relax – its just part of the cover story,' Steffi grinned.

Jenny's place looked a lot more relaxing than Aunt Muriel's but Sean only caught a fleeting glimpse of it as almost immediately they were on their way to Dublin. It took just over an hour to get to the outskirts, but then they hit serious traffic a few miles from the Meethook.

'Wow, this place is packed,' Sean exclaimed. 'Where do they all come from?'

'Told you Hot-Lads were the best group in the world,' Jenny said. She was clutching a small doll of the main singer tightly to her chest. And this was the person they were relying on to give them an alibi? Oh, deary deary me, Sean thought.

'They're not the best,' he said casually, 'they're just the most popular. There's a *big* difference.'

'You don't say?' Steffi chipped in.

'C'mon, Dad,' Jenny leaned over with a bit of over panic. 'Foot down or we're gonna be late!'

'Do you want me to fly? There are cars in front of me.'

'Then maybe we should get out and walk in?'

'Hang on. Stay in the car until we get into the car park. Or at least close to it.'

Sean shuddered. *Please* don't let us bump into someone who knows me...

It must have taken them at least half an hour to do the last mile. Hoards of teenage girls passed by, squealing like excited chickens and carrying banners with Hot-Lads printed on them.

Suddenly, Jenny pointed and shouted, 'Hey look – it's that moron off the telly!'

Sean and Jenny both turned round. Sean frowned and said, 'Who?'

'You know, that guy from the survivor game show. He got kicked off on the first day. Joseph.'

Suddenly, Sean shivered. 'Kerr!' he exclaimed.

'I thought he was brilliant!' Steffi said unexpectedly. 'I'm gonna call over!'

'No!' But before Sean could stop her, Steffi had rolled down the window. 'Hey, Joseph!' she yelled. 'Saw you on telly – you were the best!'

Much to Sean's horror, Kerr and the teenager he was with came over to the car. He gave a modest smile. 'Well, you know how it is with these jungle games. The brightest are always go first, sacrificed in favour of the more popular second-raters. I really don't think I could have taken it much longer anyway.'

He looked into the car where Sean was trying to shrink into the upholstery.

'Well, if it isn't young Mr Redmond. Strange, I didn't think you'd have the same musical tastes as my young niece here,' Kerr went on, indicating the teenager he was with.

The traffic moved on and Sean sat back feeling completely mortified.

'You know him?' asked Steffi.

'Yeah, he's one of my teachers. Complete jerk.'

'You kidding?' Steffi insisted. 'He was cool!'

'He doesn't teach you,' Sean replied.

The road turned to the left and the Meethook appeared in the distance.

'Okay, you guys, out,' said Jenny's dad. 'See you back at the house tomorrow night.'

'Okay!' The three of them bailed out, the car turned down a side alley and was gone. Sean and Stephanie flowed with the crowd for a few hundred yards and, promising to meet up again the following night at Jenny's cousin's place, crossed over the river and headed for the bus stop.

'So what does Troy look like then? I mean *really* look like?' Stephanie asked suddenly.

'Well, for a start, he's smaller than I am. And about a year and a half younger. Beyond that, black hair... baseball cap... blue eyes... You'd have liked him if he was a bit older.'

'He might not get to be a bit older when I get my hands on him,' Steffi laughed.

The bus pulled up at the seafront, and they headed to the lifeguard's hut at the far end of the beach and settled in for a bit of a wait. Fortunately, Steffi had come prepared. She opened her backpack and produced a large bottle of orange and enough chocolate to feed a small third-world nation.

13 The Vigil

It felt like hours but it was actually only about twenty minutes later when Troy, Niamh and Vinnie appeared at the end of the pier.

'Which one's Troy?' Steffi asked. 'Or do I need to ask?'

'Small one in the middle,' Sean replied.

'Thought so,' Steffi said. 'He's hanging behind the others a little.'

When they met up, Sean made the necessary introductions. Troy did actually look a little bit sheepish – unusual for him – but Steffi didn't do anything worse than give him a dig in the ribs and a pretend-angry smile.

'Did you bring everything?' Sean asked them.

'Sure did, dude,' Vinnie replied. 'Two torches this time, one digital camera to get some evidence with, Niamh has her mobile phone... did we miss anything?'

Only our common sense, Sean thought. 'Might as well get going,' he said a little nervously.

As they walked up the road that led to Clifftop House, Sean wondered, for about the hundredth time, if what they were doing was a good idea.

It was slowly beginning to dawn on him that

he did not know what he wanted from summer. Or life for that matter. When he didn't have what he wanted, he felt like he couldn't live without it. Then, when he finally did get it, he didn't want it any more. How could he be so inconsistent?

But this time, he thought, I'm right to want out. This wasn't just adventure; this was waving a large 'DANGER' sign in front of him.

The conversation trailed off as they got near the house. They slipped in behind the stunted trees and bushes on the land side of the road, crouching down as they rounded the last twist in the road.

But they weren't the only visitors to Clifftop House that night!

The black car stood in front of the gates, which were now closed – maybe padlocked into the bargain. There was nobody inside.

'Well, that's one problem solved,' said Steffi. 'They're in the house. We'll just have to wait here until they come out. If they start loading anything into the car, we'll split and call the police.'

'Might be an idea if we got ourselves better cover,' said Sean. 'They might send a look-out to check that the coast is clear.'

'Good thinking, dude,' Vinnie replied. He pulled out a small but impressive-looking camera and took a couple of shots of the car.

'Wow! Where did you get that?' Troy was clearly impressed.

'LA, man,' said Vinnie.

'You sure the pics will come out okay?' Sean said. 'The car is a bit far away and it's not all that bright.'

'Zoom lens, dude,' said Vinnie. 'And it's a digital camera so we can brighten them up when we download them on to Niamh's computer.'

'How strong is the lens?' asked Steffi.

'Times four. Should be enough.'

'We could hide behind those rocks,' Sean said, pointing to a couple of large rocks under a tree. They were well shadowed and anyone looking over at them wouldn't even see the rocks, let alone anyone hiding behind them.

'Looks okay to me, dude – let's go.'

They sneaked back under cover of the hanging branches of the trees and settled in among the rocks.

'But how are we going to find out what they're doing without going into the house,' asked Troy after about five minutes.

Sean could have killed him.

'No way. Do you really want to get nailed?' Steffi asked. 'All we have to do is wait and see what they come out with and get some photos.'

'And what if they come out with nothing?' asked Niamh.

'Oh they'll come out with something. I guarantee you.'

They all looked at her. Nobody asked exactly how she knew this. Yet they all felt that it made sense. Something was going on and sooner or later someone was going to have to come out of the house. They just had to wait.

Half an hour passed. The sun was setting behind them and midsummer twilight was beginning to fall. A sliver of a moon brightened the sky, but it didn't throw much light. At one point Steffi crawled off into a clump of bushes. When she came back, she was putting her mobile back into her pocket.

'Who on earth were you phoning?' asked Sean. 'This isn't the time for chatting!'

'Sorry. Just Jenny. Wanted to see how the gig was going.'

Sean could only look at her speechlessly.

'How much longer are we going to have to wait?' grumbled Troy. 'I would have thought that they'd want to get out of the place as soon as possible.'

'Relax,' said Niamh. 'You're too impatient.'

'Hold on,' said Sean. 'Let's work this out. High tide is ten or thereabouts. They would have to get to the house and exchange signals. Then the dinghy would set out for from the boat for the cave. Give it fifteen minutes. The stuff has to be carried up the steps. They should be out any minute now.'

The minutes ticked by. Still no one appeared.

'You don't think there's another way out of the place, do you?' asked Steffi.

'That they might have already blown the joint?' asked Vinnie.

The thought had occurred to Sean, But the car was still there. For a quick getaway. He frowned at it. But why hadn't they turned it round so that they could take off immediately? Some sixth sense was at work, telling him that something was wrong. He had this overpowering feeling that nothing was going to happen here.

Suddenly it struck him.

'We're in the wrong place,' he said.

14 The Cove

Vinnie was the first to react. 'What do you mean?' he frowned.

'I don't think we're in the right spot,' Sean repeated.

'We have to be,' said Niamh, just a little impatiently. 'They unload the stuff in the cave, bring it up the steps to the house and load it into the car.'

'It's something about the beach,' said Sean slowly. Something was tugging at his memory. Suddenly he remembered Grandad on the beach talking about the smugglers. It had stuck in his mind and he had asked some time later – during one of those lengthy Scrabble breaks – whether or not the caves were still in use.

Grandad had shaken his head. 'Couldn't be done now,' he said, 'the caves wouldn't be big enough. Over two centuries worth of sand will have blown into the cave. You wouldn't be able to get anything bigger than an inflatable in there now.'

He was right, too. Sean kicked himself for not having noticed that the cave was so shallow the night he was down there. He turned to the circle of faces before him and said, 'They'd have to make too many trips to make it worthwhile. But they can get into the cove at high tide. It's only round the corner. And then there's the car?'

'What about the car?' Niamh asked.

'It hasn't been turned round,' Sean went on. 'If they wanted to be in and out quickly, they'd have turned it first. Have it facing out so that they could get out of here as soon as possible.'

'Maybe it's not part of the plan,' said Steffi. 'Maybe they have another one at the cove.'

'They've probably gone by now,' fretted Sean. 'High tide was nearly two hours ago.'

'Well, as we're here, I think we should have a look at the cove,' Vinny said suddenly,. 'Is it, like … far?'

'There's a pathway leading down to it,' Sean said. 'Over there, by the bushes.'

'What pathway?' Troy said. 'I didn't know there was a pathway.'

'Well you wouldn't – you're an immigrant, not a native! Remember?'

Sean led them out from behind the rocks and over to some bushes at the edge of the road overlooking the bay. He pushed a few of the branches aside and opened up a small gap. He hadn't been up here recently and it was more overgrown than he remembered.

'You're sure there's a path?' Troy asked.

'Positive. I've been down it. Come on!'

The first part was tough going and blackberry brambles tore at their clothes. Sean found a broken part of a branch, which helped a little to clear the path, but he could feel the others growing more sceptical by the minute. Every now and again there'd be an 'Ouch' or a 'What was *that?*' from someone behind him.

'Well the smugglers certainly didn't come this way,' said Niamh at one point.

'No,' replied Sean. (Would this sodding jungle ever end?) 'They wouldn't have needed to. They only used the house for signalling. They'd store the stuff somewhere else.'

Then suddenly, there was the cove.

'Quick,' Sean whispered. 'Everyone down and don't make a sound.'

The five of them crouched down and peered out through the leaves. At the water's edge where the pier finished was a small concrete apron and beyond it the old disused boathouse. A shabby van was drawn up beside it. A few boats were rocking on the high water. One was tied up by the pier. The place was deserted, except for a solitary old man walking his dog.

'Maybe I should get a few shots of the van,' Vinnie said suddenly.

'Hold on a mo,' Niamh said suddenly, 'something is happening...'

The five of them looked up. Two men came out of the boathouse carrying some boxes. They loaded them into the car and then went back into the boathouse.

'Bingo,' muttered Troy.

'Exactly,' Vinnie replied. He crouched down even further behind the bushes. 'Gotta get some good photos of that van.'

'Should we call the police?' asked Sean.

'But we don't know they're doing anything illegal,' Niamh objected. 'These men could be fisherman loading fish boxes into a battered old van? They'll probably be gone by the time the police get here. We'd look just as silly as when we said we were ghost hunting. We'd really be in trouble this time.'

Sean found himself nodding. The last thing he wanted was his mother coming to a police station to pick him up in the middle of the night and making a scene. He could almost hear her: 'But my son is in Dundalk, not in Five Rivers.'

Where would she send him in that case? he wondered.

The men came out with more boxes as the man with the dog walked by and waved at them.

'There you are,' Niamh said. 'Told you they were just locals loading up some fish. Even he knows them.'

'Come on, let's get out of here,' Sean said.

'I still need a shot of the car number,' said Vinnie. 'We're head on. I want an angle.'

'We don't all need to wait here,' said Steffi unexpectedly. 'If they really are smuggling something, they've probably got someone on look-out, waiting to nab us once the van gets away. We'll have to split. Vinnie has to stay, he has the camera. And Sean as well. Niamh and I will head back up to the house.'

'What good will that do?' asked Vinnie

'Makes sense to me. Come on, Niamh.'

'What about me?' asked Troy.

There was a pause while Steffi pulled open her bag. 'Chocolate?' she said.

'Good point!' Troy conceded.

'What'll you do it there's anyone at the house?' asked Sean.

'We're not going in – just hiding out where we were before. Come up as soon as you get a picture of the number plate, okay?'

And with that they shuffled off leaving Vinnie and Sean huddled in the bushes, watching the two men coming out for a third time and loading more boxes into the van.

'Just had an idea,' whispered Vinnie as soon as they were gone. 'There's a ledge up over there. I think I can get some shots of the front of the van from there.'

'I'll come too.'

'No, wait here – it's too small and two of us moving around might get some attention. Don't worry, I won't be long.'

Seconds later, Vinnie had disappeared, leaving Sean on his own in the middle of a hedge. Thanks a bunch, lads.

Now hold on a second, said the *other* Sean Redmond, a kind of inner voice that haunted him every now and again (and where the hell had *he* been all this time?). You really are losing it. Two guys doing a bit of overtime and loading some fish into an old Ford van and you're getting freaked out? Even that guy with the dog seemed to know who they were. Poor Vinnie – he's going to look a prat if his holiday photos turn out to be a couple of locals and a car taken in dodgy light. Even if he can brighten them up later.

But hang on a second – this is Five Rivers. Everyone waves at everyone else, whether they know them or not.

He was interrupted in his internal chat when the muscle in one of his legs decided to cramp up. For a second he felt as though it was trying to twist itself inside out. He rubbed it, but that did nothing, so he tried to stand up and straighten it, letting out a little groan as he did.

Finally, the pain died away and he managed to relax a bit.

Okay, he thought, had anyone seen him? If

they had, just try to act casually. There's no law against me being here. Couldn't sleep, went out for a midnight stroll, no law against it, is there? He got up and was about to stroll back up the path to the house when a pair of powerful arms grabbed him. Something dark was slipped over his head and a hand was clamped over his mouth. He was half dragged over to the boat-house, pushed up some steps and dumped on a hard floor. A door slammed.

The engine of the van was revved up and then it drove off.

Sean took off the head covering and took a deep breath of air. Once again, he was alone, and once again he was sitting on a cold floor with nowhere to go and nothing to do in the middle of the night. *Déjà vu*, he thought they called it.

So what now? Wait until Vinnie came down to get him out?

Ha! Fat chance! Vinnie would probably be sitting in Sheridans by now, proudly down-loading photos on to Niamh's computer and telling them all about how brave he'd been and, no, he didn't know where Sean had got to – probably went home after the crooks left. Any more of those toasted-cheese sandwiches, dude...?

Speaking of food, Sean suddenly realised just how hungry he really was. It was hours since they'd had that chocolate. He was going to kill them all when he saw them again. Only for his fear that Vinnie was going to call him chicken, he could have called the police in. Who cared what Vinnie thought, anyway? He was only here for the summer.

He tried to ease himself up into a more comfortable position, only realising then how much his hip hurt. Still, at least the cramp had gone, even if the cure was worse than the malady.

His eyes slowly began to adjust the light in the boathouse. It was a surprisingly bright night given the bit of moon that was shining through a small hole in the roof. Not that there was much to look at. An outboard motor, nets, lobster pots, coils of rope, none of which seemed to have seen the water recently, and several boxes marked 'fish'. What sort of fish did they catch around here, anyway? Mum was always complaining about the difficulties in getting fresh fish in Five Rivers. So much so that Sean almost suggested she take up fishing herself.

All of the boxes here, though, seemed to be empty. They didn't even have that strong, lingering, fishy smell that always made his eyes water. Maybe they were the result of some sort of new EU directive – smell-free fish and brand new boxes for every batch.

No, there was no such directive, he thought

suddenly, and if there was no lingering fish smell it was because *these boxes were never meant to contain fish.*

So Vinnie had been right. There *were* secrets in small towns. This one, anyway. And *he* had been right about where and when the smugglers actually brought the stuff in. Somehow it only deflated him to find out how right they'd been.

He was interrupted by a gentle knock on the door. 'You in there, dude?'

Vinnie!

'Yes! I'm in here! For sod's sake get me out!'

'How'd you get in?'

'I was out for a midnight stroll, what do you think?' Sean replied sarcastically. 'They found me in the bushes and some guy dragged in here before they drove off. Can you get in?'

'I don't think so, man – there's a really good lock on the door.'

'What about your mobile?'

'Forgot to bring it from LA.'

'*What?*' Sean shook his head in disbelief. Typical! The latest state-of-the-art zoom lens camera, sunglasses, clothes, everything, the lot. But no mobile. For one glorious moment he and Vinnie were on level ground.

The only people in the world without a mobile.

15 Debriefing

'Well you certainly led us a fine dance,' said Detective Inspector Noonan. He had thick specs and a habit of looking over the top of them in between long pauses.

It was early afternoon on the following day and Sean, Niamh, Troy, Vinnie and Steffi were sitting in the inspector's office.

They had been driven back to their homes the previous night in a garda car – in Sean's case to a parent who didn't even know he was back in town. The garda gave strict instructions that they were not to be asked any questions by anyone and that they themselves were not to say a word – a single word – about what had happened.

Not asking questions did not come easily to Sean's Mum.

'What do you mean?' she asked, pouring out questions and comments in an incoherent stream. 'My son is brought home in a garda car – at midnight – and I'm not supposed to ask him where he was or what he was doing? He's supposed to be up in Dundalk, did you know that? What's he doing in Five Rivers? What is this all about? And,' one last dreadful thought finally stopping her in her tracks, 'is he in any kind of trouble?'

'Now, Mrs Redmond,' said Garda Power, 'hold on. He's not in any trouble. He and a few friends of his were merely helping us with some enquiries.'

'Oh my God, he's been arrested,' Mum wailed. 'He'll be up in court. I'm sure it was those awful Sheridans...'

'Nothing of the sort,' assured Garda Power. 'You'll hear all about it tomorrow, but until he meets the Inspector he's not to say a word about what happened to anyone.'

'Of course,' Grandad interrupted, 'I'll see to it.'

Sean crawled away upstairs, the sound of voices finally ceasing as he shut the bedroom door.

A short time later, Grandad poked his head around the door.

'Well? What was it like? The drive in the garda car? Did they have the sirens on? Lights flashing?'

'In the middle of the night...?'

'Of course.' Grandad sounded visibly deflated. 'Always wanted a drive in a garda car. Lights, sirens, the whole bag of wine gums.'

'I'll see what I can do,' Sean replied.

Mum was next. Sean braced himself for the worst, but all she said was, 'Sure you're all right?'

'I'm fine,' Sean replied. 'Just tired.'

The door closed.

Now it was the next day, a 'debriefing' session as Garda Power grandly called it.

'You could have fouled up the whole operations,' said the inspector.

'We didn't mean to,' said Niamh. 'We just felt something was going on and we all thought you wouldn't believe us if we went to you.'

'Not after the last time,' put in Troy.

'The time they said they were ghost-hunters,' explained Garda Power.

'Ah yes,' said the inspector. 'And what you doing there that night?'

'Sean here thought he saw a light in Clifftop House...'

'I did!' Sean said, rather indignantly.

'...and Vinnie did too,' continued Niamh. 'We had just read about the drug haul in the midlands and thought they might be connected.'

'Should have contacted us *before* you did anything.' Inspector Noonan looked at them over his glasses.

'Did *you* know about the lights, sir?' Vinnie asked.

'Yes. We knew drugs were bring dropped off somewhere along the coast so all stations were on high alert. We had figured that the drop would take place at high tide, so when our look-out reported lights at Clifftop House...'

Vinnie and his mega-torch, Sean thought.

'...we were puzzled. That night it wasn't high tide, you see. But we had to check it out just to be sure. And what did we find?'

'A bunch of kids who said they were looking for ghosts,' Troy said.

'Exactly. Between you and the tramp, there were days when we seemed to be chasing our own tails.'

'The tramp,' asked Sean. 'Was he connected with the smugglers?'

'No, he's just a harmless old chap who spends his time on the road mostly. Takes up residence in Clifftop when he's in town.'

'Cool!' Vinnie sounded regretful. 'I'd love to have talked to him.'

'But yesterday night... How did you know that that would be the night that something was going to happen?' Sean asked.

'As I said, we've been on special alert at times of high tides for the last few weeks. But we hadn't really worked out when and where the drugs would be landed. Then we got a mysterious call. A young voice. Hard to tell if it was a boy or a girl.'

They all looked at each other, but it was only when Sean turned to Steffi that he detected a slight flush of colour.

'Then, last night, there were another two calls. One was about the cove. Someone had worked *that* out.'

Niamh shot Sean another glance.

Why look at me? he thought. *I* couldn't have made the calls last night. Of course it was Steffi. The first that time she said she was phoning Jenny to find out how the gig was going. And the second when we were ploughing down to the cove.

'So, to conclude, we pulled out all the stops. We had a car near Clifftop House. Another where the cliff road joins the main road into town and a third at the top of the cove road, cutting off all access.'

'What about the smugglers?' asked Troy. 'Who were they?'

'Couple of young lads from the next county. Moved to Dublin but would know the whole area around here well. They may or may not be the guys who actually unloaded the drugs from the boat. Their job could just have been to answer the signals, collect the drugs from the boathouse and drop them off at a prearranged spot ... couriers they're called, by the way, not smugglers.'

'Will you ever find out?' asked Sean.

Another glance over the specs. 'We'll try. But these operations are done in compartments. one lot doesn't know how the others operate. But this will be end end of the line for these guys.

'Why?' asked Troy.

'Once they're caught, the big guys in Amsterdam and Dublin don't want them any more. They'll have been in jail and have a record. Be known to the police. There's only one rule for couriers: keep a low profile. Never do anything to draw attention to yourself, never get caught with drugs on you – dump them if necessary. That way, you avoid being questioned.'

Steffi would have made a good courier, Sean thought to himself. Keep a low profile and give away nothing. Look at how she managed to call the guards without giving away a single hint.

'About the car,' he said suddenly, remembering, 'the car with the dent in the side – that was theirs, wasn't it? We saw it parked befoe Clifftop House. It nearly ran us over once. Grandad was going to call you.'

'Pity he didn't. We would have kept an eye out for it. Asked the driver a few questions.'

'Wasn't very smart of them,' Niamh said. 'A bashed-up car nearly running people down.'

'Exactly! But then not all couriers are perfect. That's why we manage to pick them up. This pair certainly weren't. Putting anything down on paper is a bad mistake, but leaving it lying around is unforgivable. Lucky their bosses won't get to hear about it.'

So Steffi had told the police about the notebook. No wonder they took her seriously.

A tray arrived with steaming mugs of coffee. Perfect for a hot summer's day, thought Sean. Surely even a police station had a cold-drink machine somewhere.

'Well, now that we've wrapped everything up,' beamed Inspector Noonan, 'let me conclude by saying thank you all for your help. Inadvertent though it was. Mind you, you shouldn't have gotten involved at all. In future, if you have any suspicions, come to us. We're talking crime here – and it's not your job to get involved. And, by the way, if anyone ever sidles up to you in an airport and asks you to take a parcel containing milk powder for his dear old Grandma that someone will collect at the other end... get to hell out of it.'

But one thing still bothered Sean. 'That night I saw the lights. That wasn't high tide.'

'No, the lights you saw weren't made by the smugglers. They use a more powerful beam. Probably the tramp had a torch and was flashing it around.'

What about Vinnie's lights? Sean wanted to ask. Had Vinnie seen anything? Or did he just say that to keep the smuggler story alive? He decided not to ask.

'What will we tell Matt and Olwyn?' Niamh broke in.

'Simply that you noticed lights, informed us and that we went into action.'

'What about last night? When we were out so late?' Sean wanted to know.

'Well, you're an inventive bunch. I'm sure you'll think of something.'

'Like ghost-hunting,' said Vinnie.

'Yeah, that's it – ghost-hunting!'

'This is the evening news with Orlagh McGoohan. A drugs haul has taken place near Dublin early this morning. Police acting on sources swooped in the Five Rivers area and captured a sizeable amount of cannabis. The drugs were...'

'I still can't believe it,' Mum cooed. 'Cannabis. Here in Five Rivers.'

'Why not?' answered Grandad. 'Has to come in somewhere. Doesn't just drop out of the sky on to the nearest motorway.'

'...believed to have come from the Nether-lands,' droned on the newsreader.

'Detective Inspector Noonan appeared on the screen and said exactly what she had said, being very careful to add not a single item of new information.

'What caused you to think that the drop was being made in the Five Rivers area?'

'We were on alert for some time now and an

anonymous phone-call was received, giving us a tip-off.'

'That fellow is a mine of information,' grumbled Grandad.

'Anonymous phone call,' Mum said suspiciously to Sean. 'That was you, wasn't it?'

'What makes you think it was me?' Sean said. He didn't point out that it couldn't have been him because he, unlike everyone else, *didn't have a mobile!*

Mum didn't really think it was him and began complaining. 'I still can't understand exactly what the whole thing is about. Something is happening and I'm deliberately being kept in the dark here. One minute you're supposed to be in Dundalk and the next you're here, in spite of my express orders. Aunt Muriel is furious with you, by the way. And with Steffi.'

'Leave the lad be,' said Grandad. 'You're always at him. Remember he isn't the only person in this family who's disobeyed their parents.'

Mum went rather red and muttered something inaudible.

'It's very kind of you to let me stay for a week or so, Aunt Veronica,' said Steffi.

It had been assumed, rather than said, that Sean would not be returning to Dundalk immediately.

'You'll be lost without your computer,'

Grandad said to Steffi.

'Not at all. Why do you think that all this generation is interested in is getting home so that we can stay glued to a computer? There are internet cafés, you know. Anyway, we're planning a brill time with Niamh, Troy and Vinnie.'

Mum opened her mouth and then shut it. She said something about supper and disappeared.

'Now,' said Grandad reaching behind the cushion of his chair and pulling out something. 'I have a bit of a surprise for you. That fellow – Noonan, isn't it? – gave it to me. Said he'd heard you hadn't got one.'

He pulled out one of the most modern-looking mobile phones Sean had ever seen in his life.

'Games, internet access, voice recognition, everything,' said Steffi. She added in a whisper, 'They know it was you, about the cove. They asked me what you'd like.'

'Wow!' said Sean.

When Mum called them into supper she was beaming.

'I've just been phoning a few friends,' she announced. 'Telling them that Sean helped the police with the drugs haul.'

They all looked at her in horror.

'Don't worry, every one of them is sworn to secrecy. Not one of them will breathe a word about it.'

Oh, great, thought Sean. Knowing what they can do what they have no information, God only knows what they'll do when they have the complete spin on Something That Has Actually Been On The News.

He was still clutching his mobile. Mum hadn't screamed at the sight of it so presumably she'd been – what was the word? – *briefed* about it. It was about to go into action. Steffi had just shown him how to punch in the numbers. He'd call Troy and Niamh first – right after supper.

Grandad smiled at him. 'I give you three days before you've wasted all the credit in it.'

Circle of Daredevils

Meet the Daredevils.
The five who dream up mad dares.

Keith: Smooth (a little too smooth). Everyone's popular guy. Has a thing about Niamh.

Niamh: Golden girl. Goes her own way. Doesn't like to be taken for granted.

Troy: Niamh's young brother. Same airy attitude. Same sunny outlook. Can be pig-headed.

Cara: Small, spiky-haired, determined, loyal. X-ray eyes. No one fools Cara.

Sean: Determined to be part of the scene. Terrified he won't make it. Hates the piano. Thinks he loves Niamh.

Five dares. Four succeed. One fails.
There's a crunch showdown involving an island on a remote strand around which, at high tide, the water comes in faster than a galloping horse...